PUS
JUNKIES

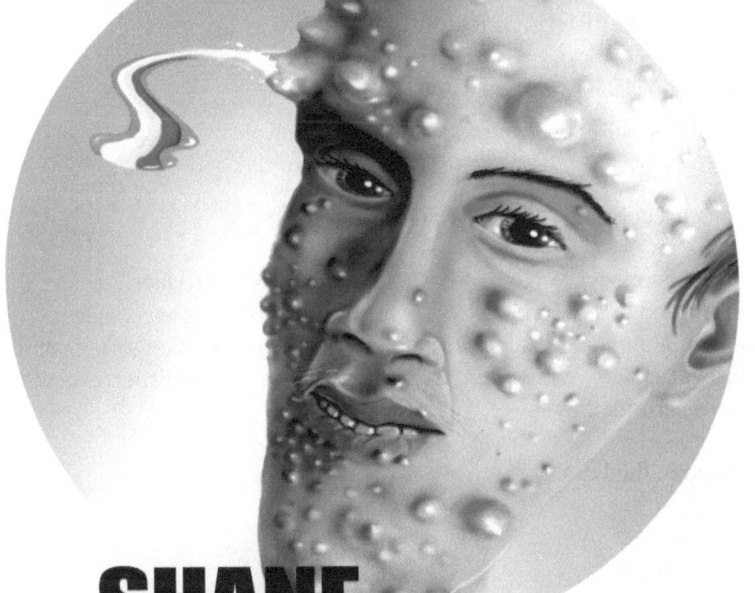

SHANE
MCKENZIE

ERASERHEAD PRESS
PORTLAND, OREGON

ERASERHEAD PRESS
205 NE BRYANT
PORTLAND, OR 97211

WWW.ERASERHEADPRESS.COM

ISBN: 1-62105-136-6

Printed in the USA.

Acknowledgements

I tend to always thank the same people. So, everyone who has been thanked before, thanks again! This is my first bizarro book, so I want to thank all of the amazing people I have had the privilege of meeting and spending time with the last two years at BizarroCon. You guys are the shit! And of course, thank you Jeff Burk, Carlton Mellick, and Rose O'Keefe. You guys push me, force me out of my comfort zone, and consistently inspire me. Love you guys. And thanks to my wife Melinda for not divorcing me when I told her my next book was called *Pus Junkies*.

For Edward Lee.

Thank you for setting the bar.
And for the term peckersnot.

CHAPTER ONE

The pus oozed out like a pale worm. Little by little, curling like a pig's tail as it spiraled out. Kip used both thumbnails to squeeze the irritated, bloated zit that had made itself at home on the spot right between his eyes. Tiny hairs stuck out of it, making it look like an oily red hedgehog on his face.

Once the pus had run out, the blood followed right behind it, painted the edge of his nails red. Kip ripped another sheet of Kleenex from the box beside him, wiped the pus string onto it, then used it to sop up the blood. He already had four torn pieces pasted to various spots on his face.

The pills weren't working. Before those, he had tried every cream and medicated ointment the dermatologist offered, every face wash and wipe he could get over the counter. The acne won the battle every time. In fact, it only seemed to be getting worse. Covering his face, the back of his neck, his chest, his ass, and his entire back. The pimples pulsated on the surface of his skin, tickled his flesh like each one was filled with baby spiders thrashing around inside.

So when none of the washes or medicated wipes worked, the doctor had given him some pills. The man had talked about how powerful they were, how they used the pills as a last resort, had some pretty serious side effects. Said Kip should see results in as little as a week or so. It had been a month. Acne still covered him like red, oily sand dunes in an endless white desert. His skin had dried out, just like the doctor said it would, but it did nothing to stop the pimples from rising. Flakes of skin like fish scales inhabited the spots between the acne, and his lips were chapped so bad they resembled twin snakes shedding their hides. He licked his finger and rubbed the dry spots on his face to moisten the skin some.

I look like a leper. How am I ever going to get laid?

7

He'd like to think that if his torso wasn't covered in pus-filled bumps that he'd have more confidence. That he would actually speak to a female—one in particular—let alone try and get one to sleep with him. That's what he told himself anyway.

With his shirt off, he lifted his arms and spun in place, keeping his eyes on the mirror. The pimples on his chest and back were inflamed, a bright neon pink, but he didn't bother popping any of them—he'd save those for later…looked forward to it. It was the ones on his face he wanted to get rid of. Not that they looked any better emptied of their white custard filling. They were now open wounds, spewing blood, the skin a darker red, almost maroon. It always took hours before the bleeding would fully stop, and then they would just become scabs attached to his skin like flattened ticks.

He got a strange kick out of popping them. There was no pain at all, but a euphoric sensation when he squeezed them. Sometimes when they got to pulsating real bad, it was almost like having an orgasm, and he'd just close his eyes and enjoy it before it passed, before the zits calmed and remained still. He was pretty sure that wasn't normal, that he probably should have said something about it to the doctor, but he never got around to it. He didn't know if it was from embarrassment or because he didn't want the doctor to make that feeling go away.

There was a new zit on his bottom lip. Even though it looked like it, the bump wasn't herpes, he knew that for sure. Had to kiss a girl to get herpes. The zit made his lip look swollen, like he'd been punched in the mouth, and no matter how hard he squeezed it, he couldn't get it to pop. It tingled, made his left eye water as it throbbed.

It's not ready yet.

He tried again anyway, rolling his eyes as the pleasure erupted across his lips. His thumbnails had carved crescent-shaped divots into the oiled flesh, and small dribbles of blood oozed out, but no pus. The zit had about doubled in size from irritation, and Kip finally decided to leave it alone.

I'll take care of it tomorrow.

8

By then it would be filled with cream, begging to be emptied out by his thumbs.

He had been trying to ignore the raised voices coming from downstairs. A few years ago, he had turned the attic into his bedroom, always thought of it as his own little hideout. Like a treehouse. His mom was totally fine with it, said he deserved it for being such a great student and an even better son.

Kip dropped to his knees, pushed down on the door just enough so he could make out what was being said.

"…trying. What the hell do you want me to do?" The voice of Kip's cousin, Zak. He'd only been living with them for about a week now.

"Get your act together, that's what. I'm doing my best here, Zak. I really am." Kip's mother. Kip could tell by the pitch of her voice that she was really upset, sounded on the verge of tears.

"I told you, I'm trying. I'm going to class and doing my best. You're tripping out this bad over a cigarette? Lady, you've got to lighten up…at least a little bit. I can't just—"

"Lady? *Lady?* You call me Aunt Jenny. You understand me? Or better yet, you call me ma'am. I will not be disrespected in my home by some punk ass kid. I'm doing you a favor here. Do you know how hard your mother begged me to bring you here? I hadn't heard my little sister cry like that since we were kids. You really did a number on her, you know that? You and that son of a bitch she's with."

"Yes. I know. And I hate that prick too. It's because of him… Look, I fucked…sorry…I *messed* up bad. I know that. I'm trying to make things right. I'm not drinking anymore. Not doing any drugs. I swear. And I'm trying hard in my classes."

Kip eased the door down a few more inches, hoping to get a glance. He could see their feet now, but didn't dare open it any further.

There was a moment of silence, and he knew his mother was covering her face with both hands and shaking her head. She always did that when she was upset.

"I don't want to catch you smoking cigarettes again.

Okay? You might not think it's a big deal, but I don't want my son seeing that kind of behavior. Deal?"

Zak sighed. "Deal. It's not like Kip'd ever actually smoke one. But I won't smoke them here."

I would too! I would if I wanted to!

"I don't like you smoking those damn things at all. But you don't do it here at my home, and we won't have a problem."

"Cool."

"And have you ever thought about asking Kip to help you with your studies? I'm sure he'd be glad to tutor you."

Kip closed the door then. He wasn't in a hurry to hear Zak's answer to that question, though he hoped his cousin would ask him for help. Zak was the closest thing Kip had to a friend, and since Zak had arrived, he hadn't said five words to Kip. When they were kids, they used to be best friends. Inseparable. When Kip found out Zak was coming to live with them for a while, was going to go to the same high school, he had been so excited, he even cleared out a space in his room for Zak to sleep.

But Zak wasn't that kid anymore. He'd changed into a completely different person. Kip hadn't seen his cousin in a long time, not since Kip was in fifth grade and Zak was in eighth. Kip remembered how impressed he was that Zak was already in middle school, on the verge of high school.

But Zak had been held back a couple of grades. Now, they were both seniors.

They used to play video games together, used to pretend to be super heroes and super villains and have epic battles. Any time there was a family get together, Kip and Zak would immediately run to Kip's room, would always groan when the night was over and Zak had to leave.

Then Aunt Sarah moved away to another state. Kip didn't know too much about it, but heard his mom saying something about a new boyfriend. Then later, Kip heard something about the new boyfriend beating up Aunt Sarah and Zak all the time. Then talks switched from the new boyfriend to Zak and how bad *he* had gotten. How he had been getting into trouble all the time, doing drugs, not going to class.

The next thing he knew, Zak was back. Living with them. A dream come true…if it was seven years ago. Now, Kip was too scared to even talk with the guy. If it was up to Kip, they would play super heroes and super villains right now in his room. He didn't care how old they were.

Kip pulled on a pair of jeans and a Captain America t-shirt. Just as he slipped his arms into the straps of his backpack, there was a knock at his door.

"Kip? Kip, honey?"

Kip checked the mirror one more time, removed the bloody Kleenex bits, tossed them into the plastic wastebasket next to the mirror, making a mental note to empty the trash later—it was overflowing with pus-encrusted tissue. He licked his fingertip and rubbed the dry blood off his face, whimpering at the euphoric sensation. He threw the door open and climbed down the pull-out stairs.

"Hey, Mom."

"Honey, I'm running late this morning. Your breakfast and lunch money are on the counter, but you're going to have to ride with your cousin to school, okay?"

Kip's face burned. "Aw, Mom. I bet he doesn't want me riding with him. Did you ask him?"

"He doesn't have a choice in the matter. It'll be fine. Why wouldn't he want you riding with you? That's ridiculous."

Because I'm the Toad. Because he's only been here for a week and he's already popular, and I'm a goddamn leper.

Kip just shrugged.

"You were so excited when you heard Zak was coming to stay with us. What's the matter now?"

Kip looked over his shoulder to make sure Zak was nowhere around. "Well…he's not the same as before. He barely even talks to me. I feel weird around him now."

"He's just getting adjusted. How would you feel if I sent you away to live with Aunt Sarah? Give it some time, I'm sure the two of you will be just like old times soon." She smiled, cupped the back of his head. "The pills are working. I can tell."

Kip made a sound like *pffft*. "Yeah right. It's worse than ever."

11

"Well…the doctor said it would get worse before it got better, right? So maybe that's what's happening."

Kip wiped at the blood on his face again, rubbed it on his jeans.

His mom checked the wall clock, arched her eyebrows. "Okay, honey. See you at dinner tonight. Have a great day." She kissed him on the forehead and then was out the door, backing down the driveway in the next minute, and then gone.

Kip trudged toward the kitchen. His breakfast was a couple of Pop-tarts and a glass of orange juice. He didn't know why his mother felt she needed to pour his juice for him every morning, but he never said anything. If it made her feel important, that was fine with him. He was getting sick of Pop-tarts, though.

Sitting at the table, he took a long gulp of juice, then bit into his cinnamon and brown sugar Pop-tart. He licked the crumbs away, tasted the bitterness of the boil on his lip, but had grown used to that flavor. Kind of liked it. A pleasure shiver ran up his spine as his taste buds massaged the zit like thousands of stubby fingers.

Then Zak walked in. He sort of hesitated when he saw Kip at the table, then put on an obviously fake smile and nodded. "Got any more of those?"

"Yeah, sure. In the cupboard next to the microwave." When Kip spoke, crumbs blew from his mouth and scattered across the table.

"Thanks, man." Zak grabbed the box, seemed to hesitate again, then finally sat at the table with Kip. The silver Pop-tart wrapper seemed louder than usual as Zak tore into it.

Kip cleared his throat, wanted to say something, but drank orange juice instead. He only ever felt this awkward around girls, but for some reason, Zak was making him uncomfortable.

"So…how've you been, Kip? It's been a long time, right?" Zak's breath smelled like cigarette smoke.

"Yeah. I was still in elementary school the last time I saw you. And I've been good I guess."

"Cool."

More silence. Kip wanted to run away.

"Look, man. I hope you don't mind me coming to stay with you guys. It wasn't my idea or anything. I kind of fucked up back home, and Mom didn't think there was any other way. She said if I stayed there, I'd keep fucking up. And she's right."

"No, I don't mind. Not at all. How did you...f-fuck up? Back home I mean."

"Remember when we were kids and we didn't have anything to worry about except comic books and video games?"

"Yeah. Of course."

"God I miss those days. I'd give anything to be that age again." Zak absently chewed the pastry and stared at the wall. "You know we moved to California because my mom met some guy, right?"

Kip nodded.

"Ernie...and he's a fucking dick. Gets off on hitting my mom and me. It's because of him. All this shit is because of him."

Kip didn't know what to say so he just bit into the second Pop-tart.

"I come home from school one day, right? Mom's still at work. This motherfucker is there waiting on me. Drinking liquor and smoking weed. And he sat me down and made me do it with him. Said if I didn't, he'd kick my ass."

"Really? God...that sounds awful."

Zak shrugged. "Anyway, I kind of liked it. I didn't tell Mom about it, thought she'd get mad at me instead of him. Then I started sneaking into their room when they weren't there, drinking, smoking, taking pills. It got bad. School didn't matter anymore to me. It's weird. I don't remember some parts, and there's things my mom says I did and said to her that I don't remember at all." Zak laughed, finished off his food. "And here I am. Mom says you and Aunt Jenny are good for me. And you know what? She's probably right. I don't want to do those things anymore, man. I want...fuck. Nevermind."

"No. What do you want?"

Zak reached over and punched Kip in the shoulder. Kip could tell his cousin was trying to be playful, but it still hurt a little. He did his best not to grimace.

"I want to be more like you. I want to be like I was when I was a kid, you know? I hate who I am now. I don't wanna be like that fucking douchebag back home."

He wants to be like me? Really?

As much as Kip wanted to keep talking with Zak, the clock told him that they needed to be out of the door soon if they were going to make it to class on time.

"Think we need to get going," Kip said through a mouthful of half-chewed pastry.

"Yeah. Okay. About that." Zak rubbed the back of his head, pinched one eye shut, and hissed. "Any chance I could get out of taking you to school today?"

Kip chewed as fast as he could, swallowed. "Are you serious? After everything you just said, you're still going to skip class?"

"No, no, no. I'm not skipping. It's just…there's this girl. I'm supposed to pick her up today, and…well…kinda wanna be alone with her, know what I mean?"

"Oh. Yeah…yeah, I get it." Kip did his best not to look like a dork, but knew he was failing miserably. "Think you can at least get me close by? Even if I start walking right now, I'd still be late."

"Yeah. Yeah I can do that."

"Thanks. And you're going to class, right?"

"Yes, mother. I'm going to class. But this girl…she's killer, man. You know who Jade—"

"Jade? Jade Brewster?"

No way. He's been here for a week, and he's already with the hottest girl in school?

"I guess. She never told me her last name."

"Sh-she's the only Jade in the school. How did you…I mean… How?"

Zak smiled, lightly slapped Kip on the back of the head. "You haven't changed much since we were kids, have you, Kip? Like…at all."

Kip's face burned red and he could feel his acne start to frenzy like cooking pig flesh. "Yes I have."

"How?" They were out the door now, walking toward Zak's car. It was old-looking, covered in rusty blotches that reminded Kip of his own skin.

"Lots of things. I turned the attic into my room. It's pretty cool, you should come see."

"That's not what I mean, Kip. I'm just gonna come out and ask. You ever had any pussy?" Zak was in the driver's seat now, twisting his fists over the steering wheel and smiling up at Kip as he entered the car. "Ever kissed a girl at least?"

Kip lost his footing and slammed his chest into the passenger seat, his backpack swinging up and slapping him in the back of the head. He cleared his throat, couldn't look his cousin in the eye anymore.

"I think that answers my question, cousin. It's cool, man. Can I ask why not?"

The car was parked against the curb, and they took off toward school.

"I don't know. I can't talk to girls. I mean…look at me. You know what they call me?"

Zak pursed his lips, widened his nostrils. Kip could tell he already knew. It was probably Jade that told him. But Zak shook his head.

"They call me Toad. Because of my pimples, they say I look like a toad covered in warts. How am I supposed to get a girlfriend with a nickname like that?" Kip felt like crying, but concentrated hard not to.

"You know they got pills for that now, right?"

"Yeah. I've been taking them for like a month. It's like my acne is from another planet or something. It can't be killed! Super-human pimples. It's weird."

Zak reached over and patted Kip on the knee. "We're teenagers, cousin. Lots of teenagers have acne, it's no big deal. You can still get a girl if you have pimples. Even if your nickname is Toad. I promise you."

"Yeah? How?"

"Confidence. You have to show them that none of that

15

shit bothers you. That even though you have zits or whatever, even though they call you Toad…you don't care. You have to show them that you are the man and you know it. Girls eat that shit up."

Kip sighed. "Yeah, that's easy for you to say. I can't do that. No way."

Zak stared at the side of Kip's head for a minute, but didn't say anything. Kip couldn't look at him, was too embarrassed. He checked his reflection in the side mirror, wished he could just grab hold of his face and rip it off like a mask. Then maybe a knew one would grow. One that looked more like Zak.

Or anyone else.

The car stopped.

"All right, Kip. Jade's house is just down the street. Sorry, man. About making you walk. I'll make it up to you, all right? You won't tell your mom or anything, will you?"

"Don't worry about it." Kip hopped out and started walking. It would probably take him a good fifteen minutes to get there, and he would have to run straight to class to make it in time. But at that moment, he was glad to get out of Zak's car. Didn't want to talk about his inability to attract the opposite sex anymore.

"I promise, Kip. I'll make it up to you. Maybe we can hit a movie or something, yeah? Just me and you."

Kip couldn't keep his mouth from rising into a smile. "Yeah? That'd be cool. Street Trash is playing at the Alamo right now. I was wanting to go. Is tonight okay?"

Zak obviously had never heard of the film. Kip liked old corny horror movies as much as he liked his video games and comic books.

"Yeah, sure. See you later, cousin."

"See you at school, right?"

"Yes, yes. I'll be there. And, uh…Kip? You think maybe, I mean if I need it or whatever…that you might be able to help me with some things? Homework, studying for tests… that kind of thing?"

Kip's grin nearly ate his entire face.

"If I need it," Zak repeated.

"No problem. I'd like that."

"Cool."

They stood there for an awkward moment, Kip smiling stupidly at his cousin.

"All right then. See you later," Zak said, then was off down the road.

Jade Brewster. Wow.

Kip started walking toward school, but his walk became a trot as his excitement burst out of him. It was the first time in a long time that he actually felt like he had a friend.

His zits boiled and vibrated, filling him with ecstasy.

Poor kid.

Zak felt bad for Kip, though he wasn't lying when he said he wanted to be more like him. Kip had it easy, still the same old kid he always was. Just so goddamn innocent. School was second nature to him. He still found joy in things like super heroes and video games. Zak would give anything to be able to think that way.

But that acne. Jesus...

Zak had never seen anyone with acne that bad before. Each zit was big enough to have its own brain. And they looked painful, like every facial expression must be agonizing. He could tell Kip picks at them too, with all the scars and dark spots on his skin. A few of them had been bleeding, little red beads swelling at the tips.

And Zak could have sworn he saw them move. When Kip was in the passenger seat and Zak was asking him about girls. It was like they were bulging out, almost like they were breathing.

Just the sunlight hitting them weird. That's all.

And the kid said all the other kids call him Toad. Actually, Jade had told him about it the other day. "You're Toad's cousin? Seriously?"

That's so fucked up. Zak wouldn't let that shit stand, not while he was around. Kip was a good kid, always had been, and he was the last person that deserved that kind of treatment.

17

He knew every school, every grade, had their *Toad*. The kid everyone else picked on to make themselves feel better.

But not Kip. Not anymore. They can find someone else.

When he pulled the old Corolla up to Jade's house, she was leaning against her front door smoking a cigarette. She wore a short black skirt that hung down just above her knees, with white stockings covering her long legs. Curls of smoke billowed from her fat, pink lips. She stomped her cigarette out, then crossed her arms, mashing her breasts together, deepening her light brown cleavage.

Zak's pulse quickened, but he remained calm. Cool. He had only known this girl for a few days, and though she was definitely hot, he could already tell this girl had some crazy in her. She reminded Zak of himself, the old Zak anyway, and that scared him.

"What's up?" she said as she slid into the passenger seat. She leaned over the middle console, both of her tits pressing up against Zak's forearm. Her lips found his ear, and as she kissed, lightning shot down Zak's spine. Then she found his mouth with her tongue and his crotch with her hand.

Her caress felt damn good, if not a little rough, but Zak pulled away from her, sort of chuckled. "Whoa. Happy to see me?"

She looked stunned, her mouth hanging open. "What the fuck is your problem, man?"

"What? Just chill out, all right?" Zak tensed up for a minute as she stared him down with venom in her eyes, but then her face softened and she smiled, bit her thumbnails.

This girl is trouble. Big trouble.

"So where we going?" she said, pulling a small bottle of lotion from her purse. She squeezed a worm of the pink stuff into her hand, rubbed her palms together, and released the smell of raspberries into the car. She pulled up her skirt—flashing the crotch of her hot pink panties, her pussy lips chewing on the fabric—rolled her stockings down, and ran her hands across the pale flesh of her legs.

"Um…we're going to school. Remember that place with the teachers and the learning and what not?"

"Fuck you, asshole. You don't have to be a smart ass."

Zak didn't know how to react to that. She still held that smile though. It was clear this girl was used to getting what she wanted.

"But seriously. Where're you taking me?" She squeezed more lotion onto her fingertips, ran it across the twin bulges of her tits, making them glisten in the sunlight.

Zak couldn't tear his eyes away, and he had to wipe the moisture from his lips.

"I know you like it, Zak. All the boys do. It's okay…you can touch if you want to." She sort of leaned back, one hand combing through her hair, the other fingering the collar of her shirt. "You really wanna go to school that bad? I can teach you things too. I can teach you all sorts of things."

"It's tempting…I'm serious. But I promised… I just have to go to school, okay?"

"Promised who? Your greasy little cousin? You'd pass me up because you made Toad a promise to be a good boy?" She had that twisted expression again, but she still rubbed herself, now massaging her inner thighs with both hands, biting her lower lip.

"Not just him. His mom too, my aunt. And you know what? Don't fucking call him Toad anymore. I don't like that shit." Zak finally threw the car into drive and pulled away from Jade's home, toward school.

"Are you seriously driving us to school right now?" Now she was all business. Sitting up straight, arms crossed.

"Yep. Seriously."

"Okay, okay. I'm sorry. I'm sorry I called your cousin—"

"Kip. His name's Kip."

"Kip then. I'm sorry I called him Toad. I won't anymore. Okay? Do you forgive me?" She leaned over the center console again, started at his neck. She slid her tongue over the sensitive skin, bathed it in saliva. Then her face was in his lap. And his zipper was being pulled down.

He wanted to stop her. Knew he should have. But he didn't. When her mouth engulfed him, when her tongue swirled over every inch, he could only moan, could only grab a fistful of her hair as she started bobbing up and down, up and down.

She pulled off of his cock with a loud pop, smiled up at him. "I know a place. Let's go."

Almost every part of Zak's brain told him to refuse. Told him to pull her off, shove her away, get his ass to school like he was supposed to. But he nodded instead.

He was surprised how good she was at giving directions with a mouthful of cock.

CHAPTER TWO

Lunch time. Kip hadn't seen Zak all day, had hoped they might run into each other at some point. Kip wanted the other kids to see them together, to see that Kip had cool friends. Or one cool friend anyway. He told himself he and Zak were just missing each other, that it was just bad timing. He told himself that Zak wouldn't skip class, not after their talk.

He kept smiling sporadically all day, just thinking about having his cousin at home with him. The only person he had ever really considered a friend. His best friend.

And we're going to see Street Trash tonight.

He couldn't wait. He'd seen the movie at least five times already, but never in a theater. And never with a friend. There was over two hundred bucks burning a hole in his sock drawer at home—saved from his last birthday—and though he was saving it for a new computer, he had already decided to pay for everything tonight. The movie tickets, popcorn, candy, and sodas. Or whatever else Zak wanted. Maybe they could stop for a burger and fries afterward.

Kip had bought two pepperoni pizza pockets with the lunch money his mom had left for him, and sat at a corner table alone. He flipped through the latest Deadpool comic book, being careful not to rub any grease over the pages. This was pretty much his daily ritual. Try to hide in the shadows so his fellow students wouldn't notice him.

"Hey," a voice came from across the cafeteria.

Kip recognized the voice as Chuck, the douchiest jock in the whole school. The guy played football, basketball, and was even on the wrestling team. Kip only knew that because he had two classes with the jerk, and that's all he and all his jock friends ever talked about. And of course, as if the asshole couldn't be any more revolting, he was dating the head cheerleader,

Chelsea McMahon. It was so cliché it hurt Kip's teeth.

And Chuck just loved to give Kip shit, got off on it, him and all his buddies. He was the one who dubbed Kip Toad in the first place.

There's an entire cafeteria full of kids. He's not talking to me. Just keep your head down and mind your business, Kip.

"You hear me talking to you, Toad?"

Damn.

Kip's eyes slowly rose from the comic toward the sound of Chuck's voice, and he saw that most of the other kids were looking Kip's direction now. As he felt himself blushing, his zits got to pulsating again. Felt like his entire body was thrashing in place, and it felt great. His eyelids flickered as he stared across the cafeteria at Chuck's scowling face.

Kip only locked eyes with Chuck for a second before returning his attention to the comic book. He took another bite of his food and chewed it slowly, waiting for the onslaught.

Where are you, Zak?

Part of the reason he had been so happy today was because he thought being Zak's cousin would somehow save him from all the ridicule he had been enduring for most of his life as a student. Zak was instantly popular when he arrived at Bowie High School. The girls loved him right away. Kip had heard a group of them talking, saying how Zak looked like David Beckham and that he was mysterious and they couldn't stop swooning over how hot and cute he was.

At first, Kip resented Zak for this, even though he knew damn well it wasn't his cousin's fault. But after this morning, things had started to feel like they used to, back when they were kids, back when they were best friends.

And since Zak is so popular and so...attractive to the ladies, maybe I'll become popular too. Maybe they'll finally stop teasing me and start treating me like one of their own.

"I can't tell what's greasier, Toad. Your face or your pizza pocket. I bet if I scraped the oil off your back, I could run my Mustang on it. Whattya think, Toad?"

Kip just shrugged, turned the page. Though he glanced at the pictures, he couldn't read the words. His vision was getting too blurry. Avoiding Chuck's face, he quickly glanced around the cafeteria, hoping his cousin would be there, would come to his rescue. Would charge across the cafeteria like the Incredible Hulk and smash Chuck's face into meatloaf. But he only saw the smiling faces of the rest of his classmates. And every last one of them was enjoying the show. Most probably just glad it wasn't them being picked on.

There was only one face he caught sight of that didn't look amused, and as soon as Kip saw that she was looking in his direction, listening to all the teasing, he wanted nothing more than to run away. Or die. Whichever came first.

Just seeing her sitting there, concern pinching her face, his acne throbbed more violently, felt like the pimples would start popping on their own any second, spray pus and blood all over the place.

Gwendolyn. She was the only person in the entire school, besides the staff, that was ever nice to him. He wouldn't call her a friend or anything like that. They never hung out, never really spoke that much, but every now and then she'd smile at him, talk to him a little. It was always about whatever they were learning about in class, but that was fine with Kip. She took the time to talk to him, and that was enough. It was more than enough.

Except that he knew she did it out of pity. It was written all over her face how sorry she felt for him, but it just proved to Kip how sweet she was. How perfect she was.

And she was so pretty, always smelled so good. Her scent reminded Kip of the candy store, with a hint of flowers. Like rose flavored licorice. She never wore any makeup, never dressed in anything provocative, never showed any skin. But she didn't need to. In Kip's opinion, she was beautiful, his dream girl, and seeing her sitting there across the cafeteria pitying him hurt like a shotgun wound to his chest. The zits frenzied like they were trying to tear free from his skin.

Throb...throb...throb.

Sure, Jade Brewster was drop-dead gorgeous, was probably the source of every boner in school, but if Kip had his choice, he would take Gwendolyn any day. An easy decision. He had lain in bed many nights, imagining

Gwendolyn confessing her love for him, kissing him with tears in her eyes. That was as far as his fantasy ever got, but it was wonderful. He couldn't imagine what it would be like to actually kiss her, to feel her soft lips pressed up against his, her nails scraping across his scalp as they embraced.

Jade Brewster was hot though. And she made appearances in his fantasies too, but they weren't as sweet as his Gwendolyn ones.

Now that he thought about it, he hadn't seen Jade around either. He had seen Jezebel and Sasha, Jade's clique, and they were hardly ever without her.

Zak skipped school with her. That's what he did. He lied to me. And now I'm stuck here with all of these assholes. Alone. Like always.

Kip was still hungry, but decided not to finish his food. The sickness growing like mold in his belly overpowered his hunger, and he wrapped a paper towel over the remaining pizza, tucked his comic under his arm, and stood.

"Where you going, dork? I'm not done talking to you." Chuck weaved his way through the tables toward Kip, his buddies, Cash and Jerrod, following behind like a pair of pilot fish to a great white. Kip wondered if either of them could actually think for himself. They were like moons trapped in Chuck's gravitational pull.

"Leave him alone, Chuck." Gwendolyn was on her feet now. "Does it make you feel like a big man picking on someone smaller than you?"

At the sound of her voice, after hearing her stick up for him like that, Kip had to grab the edge of the table as his acne came alive. It pulsed so hard, he wondered if any of the other kids could see his face moving, see his skin thumping like he was filled with one giant beating heart, pressing tight against his skin from the inside. Hearing Gwendolyn's tone as she stood up to Chuck, knowing why she was doing it, might have been worse than her joining in on the ridicule.

She thinks I'm pathetic. She thinks I'm a loser. And she's right.

"What, you want me to pick on you instead?" Chuck now

24

stood just in front of Kip, but had his eyes on Gwendolyn. He grabbed his crotch and licked his lips. "I gotta pick right here for you, girl. And I know you want it."

Cash and Jerrod chuckled, both still staring Kip down hard. Kip kept his eyes on the table, chancing glances at Gwendolyn every few seconds.

"You're a fucking pig. All of you are."

"What the fuck did you just say, bitch? Maybe I'll shove my dick down your throat, shut you the fuck up."

"Hey," Kip said. He was on his feet, and the sudden motion of standing tossed his chair onto its side behind him. Now all attention was back on him. Chuck's head turned slow, like an owl's, and his eyes looked like open flames on his face. "L-leave her alone, okay? If you need someone to pick on, just pick on me."

Each bead of sweat felt like it had tiny spindly legs that tickled him as they ran down his flesh. He could feel each individual pimple now, each one calling his attention all at the same time. Each one inflated and deflated like a frogs' throat.

The tingling became so intense that he started to feel his pants tighten. His erection pressed up against his cold zipper and demanded to be let free, and all Kip could do was hunch his back some and hope nobody noticed.

"What'd you say, you little faggot?" Chuck took a long step toward Kip.

Kip closed his eyes, turned his head, and awaited the fist that was surely on its way to his face. Chuck had never actually hit him before, had kept it to verbal abuse, a few shoves here and there. But Kip had never stood up to him, had always just taken it.

"What's going on in here?"

Kip's eyes burst open at the sound of Mrs. Lee's voice. One of the assistant principals. She was always nice to Kip, always making sure nobody messed with him. She shot Kip a quick smile and nodded, then turned toward the boys and scowled.

"I suggest you boys walk away before you find yourselves in the principal's office. Wouldn't it be a tragedy for you to miss the big game?" She gasped and covered her mouth, eliciting a few giggles from the other kids.

Chuck and his buddies were already backing away. Chuck kept his eyes on Kip the whole way, smiling, nodding. His friends did the same, elbowing each other and snickering.

"If I see you boys picking on Kip again, I promise your coach will be hearing about it. And I'll personally see to it that you don't play. Understand?"

Chuck and his buddies nodded, hands up in surrender.

Gwendolyn rolled her eyes, gathered her things, and stood. She shot another look toward Kip, sort of pursed her lips, then walked out the side door, the opposite direction of Chuck and his jock minions.

Kip started heading the same direction as her, not to try and talk to her, but because it seemed like the best route to avoid another confrontation. He couldn't even look at Mrs. Lee, just wanted to be out of there.

"See you later, Toad. See you real soon," Chuck said, cracking his knuckles and licking the front of his teeth. Cash and Jerrod thought this was hilarious.

Throb...throb...throb.

"What the fuck is that?" Zak blew smoke from his nostrils as he flicked the butt of his cigarette.

"Oh, come on. Don't be such a pussy, man." Jade unscrewed the top of the Crown Royal bottle, pressed it to her lips, and tilted her head back. She held it there for a few seconds before pulling it away and hissing. Then she offered it to Zak.

"No thanks. You know it's barely past noon, right?"

"So what? It's not a big fucking deal, okay?" She took another drink, then went digging around her purse again. "That's what the coke's for." A small Ziploc bag full of white powder was now pinched between her thumb and forefinger.

"Are you fucking serious right now? You're not doing that shit in my car. God...if I knew you had that..."

"Then what? You would have pulled your dick out of my mouth and told me to leave? I doubt it." She opened the bag, glancing toward Zak as she did it.

"Don't. I'm serious."

"Dude, you're totally blowing it right now. You know that?" She dipped her pinkie nail into the bag, pressed it to her left nostril, and snorted. Then she repeated for her right. Her eyes fluttered and she leaned back in her chair and moaned, smiled.

Zak started the car and started pulling out of the woods. He already hated himself for skipping school, for lying to Kip. His cousin had probably been looking for him all day, had probably already figured out Zak didn't show up.

He's gonna be pissed. I'll have to make it up to him somehow.

"Where the fuck're you going, Zak? Just chill out for a second." She checked her nose in the visor mirror, ran her tongue over the front of her teeth. "Besides…coke makes me horny. Pull over and fuck me. Right now."

"No. I'm taking you home. I can't do this. I told you that…told you I came to town to get away from that shit. And you brought fucking coke with you?"

When Zak glanced back at her, she had her shirt pulled up and her tits out. She squeezed them together and flashed Zak a painfully sexy smile.

"Come on. Can't you just have some fun…one last time? I prooooomise I'll make it worth it."

She leaned over again, and now Zak was becoming annoyed. As fine as she was—and she was damn fine—he had had enough of her. He shoved her away, hard enough so she knew he wasn't playing around. Her body slammed against the passenger door, shaking her tits and inducing a yelp.

"I bit my tongue, you fucking asshole." She pulled her shirt back down, inspected her mouth in the mirror. "I'm bleeding. I'm fucking bleeding."

Zak didn't see any blood, and he refused to apologize. He remained silent as they pulled out of the woods and drove down the road back toward her neighborhood. She cursed under her breath the whole way, shot poisonous glances toward Zak every other second it seemed.

By the time Zak pulled the car to the curb in front of her

house, the Crown Royal bottle was empty and she was in the middle of snorting another bump from her pinkie nail.

"Look, Jade. I like you and everything…but I've only been here a week. I think maybe I need to slow things down, you know? Get adjusted to all this shit before I—"

"Before you what? Fuck me again?" Her window had been down, and she threw the liquor bottle hard against the pavement, shattering it, then swung her hard eyes back toward Zak.

"Whoa. Chill out. I'm just saying that right now, I don't think I should be seeing anyone." He had his eyes on his knuckles, his hands wrapped tightly over the steering wheel. Then he looked up at her, startled at how red her face had become. "And I didn't even fuck you."

"Oh, that's right. You just let me suck your dick, right?" She shoved her fingers into her mouth, pushed her fist in as far as it would go, started making a sound like she was about to vomit. Then she shoved her fingers into her crotch, all the while baring her teeth at Zak.

"What the fuck are you doing?"

"You're fucking me, Zak. Don't I feel good?"

"Get out. Get the hell outta my car. You're fucking crazy, man."

She just widened her legs more, moaned as her hand worked at her groin. There was some white residue just under her nose, like a tiny white Hitler mustache.

Zak threw his door open, stormed around the car, opened her door, and dragged her out. By the time he had her out in the open, she had stopped fingering herself and now threw her arms like she was swatting at a swarm of attacking bees.

"Fuck you, you bastard. Don't you ever talk to me again, you hear me? You won't ever know how good I am. And I'm fucking good, man. Real good." She pushed him in the middle of the chest, retrieved her bag from the car, and stomped toward her house, shoving Zak again when she passed the second time.

"Jade—"

"Fuck you!" *Slam!*

Zak stood there staring at her door for a second before realizing he probably wasn't safe. He walked hastily back to his car, hopped in, and burned off before that crazy bitch had a chance to grab a butcher knife and come screaming back outside or something.

No matter how good looking, she wasn't worth that shit. She knew how to suck a dick though, that was for sure.

Zak tried not to think too hard about her little "you're fucking me" show she had put on. He didn't think there would be enough of his load left in her mouth for anything to happen, but then again, he couldn't be sure. The last thing in the entire universe he needed to worry about was getting some girl pregnant. And not just some girl, but that bat-shit crazy lunatic back there.

The clock told Zak that if he sped toward school, he would still have enough time to make his last two classes for the day. But then he decided it might not be the smartest idea. *What if I run into one of my teachers in the hall whose class I skipped?*

No, it would be better to just skip the entire day, make it consistent. That way if any questions were asked, he could just say he was sick. He didn't plan on skipping again, so he hoped it wouldn't be a bigger issue.

Maybe I can park somewhere close by, try and catch Kip walking home.

He lit a cigarette and found a good spot to park and wait. Not so close to the school that someone might see him, but the car was enough in the open that when Kip walked by, he'd see it. He hoped Kip wasn't too pissed. Zak had planned on telling him about the Senior Skip Day party, but if Kip was upset, maybe he'd wait until later.

His eye caught something white on the floorboard on the passenger side. Jade's little baggie lay on its side, its contents nearly completely used up. Zak's fingers shook as he reached for it, flicked it, inspected it. Nobody would know. He could just take it now, real quick, and not a soul would have a clue.

But he tossed it into the street instead.

I'm not that guy anymore. And I don't ever want to be again.

29

CHAPTER THREE

"Hey, Toad! I bet your zits are bigger than your balls, huh!"

Kip didn't even turn to see who said it. He could tell by the voice that it wasn't Chuck, and at that moment, that was all he was worried about.

He caught the usual looks, the other kids smiling and laughing at him as he passed, the quieter kids elbowing each other and whispering things, but most shouting out insults, throwing balls of paper or other harmless things. It seemed like the word *Toad* was on each and every one of their lips.

Kip balled his hands into hard fists as he stomped his way across the school parking lot and toward the street. He couldn't wait to get home. Couldn't wait to hide in his room, his treehouse, and leave all this behind him for another day. Each day felt like a small victory, though he wondered how much of a victory today had been after his run in with Chuck.

Which, of course, was nothing new, but today Chuck had a look in his eye. A look that Kip knew meant this wasn't over.

Kip hurried his walk, felt a sort of calm wash over him as he stepped off school grounds and onto the public street. But then he realized he was actually probably safer on school grounds where the staff could intervene, stop Chuck from stomping Kip's face in.

Kip checked left and right, saw that the coast was clear, and rushed down the street on his way home. Though the incident with Chuck weighed heavy on his mind, it was his cousin he was most upset about. He had really believed Zak at breakfast this morning, actually felt sorry for him.

And then after all of that, he skipped class anyway. For what? A piece of ass? Drugs?

Probably both.

Kip told himself that if he were in Zak's position, he would have blown Jade off and gone to class like he was supposed to. Then again, being in Zak's position was as much of a fantasy as galloping down a rainbow on a unicorn's back.

Can I really blame him? It's Jade Brewster for crying out loud. Staring at her tits was like staring at God...if he had tits.

Kip stopped in his tracks. Zak's car was parked up against the curb down the street, his cousin leaning against it with a cigarette smoldering between his lips.

"Oh great," Kip said under his breath. His head drooped as he walked forward, purposefully not heading toward Zak's car. He wanted the guy to know he was upset, to know that it hurt Kip that he had broken his promise to him.

Zak pushed off his car with a backwards thrust of his hips, dropped his cigarette, and stomped it out. He held both arms out as if beckoning Kip toward him for a hug.

That's when the blue Mustang came roaring down the street, from just behind Kip. The tires squealed as the car hugged the turn and then roared right for him.

Kip dove, smacked the right side of his face on the dry, hard grass next to the sidewalk. The Mustang flew by, and Kip had hoped that would be the end of it, that Chuck would be satisfied by nearly running Kip over.

But then the sportscar stopped. Both doors swung open.

"Did y'all see that Toad leap? Damn, looks like the name fits better than I thought." Chuck wore only a white muscle shirt now, tucked into his blue jeans. Cash and Jerrod followed close behind, both smiling, flexing their muscles and flaring their nostrils.

Kip struggled to get to his feet, his massive backpack weighing him down. He carried all of his books in it at all times, never used his locker. The last time he opened his locker, there was a pile of dead flies in it, and a handwritten note that said, "Bon appetite, Toad."

A tear escaped his eye and rolled down his cheek, and Kip tried to wipe it away before the boys saw it, but was too late.

"Aw. What's the matter, Toad? You were such a brave

31

man before. Remember?" Chuck rushed forward before Kip could make a run for it, grabbed him by the arms with both hands. His grip was like two pit bulls biting into the meat of his upper arms, and Kip hissed through his teeth, thought about kicking Chuck but held back, didn't want to make things worse.

The whole time, the chorus of his buddies' laughter hit Kip in bursts.

Throb...throb...throb.

"What, your girl isn't here and now you're back to being a pussy? That it, Toad? I'm disappointed, man. I was hoping you'd grown some balls overnight, but I guess your vagina is alive and well." Chuck's knee thrust upward and slammed into Kip's groin, exploding the air from his lungs and twisting his guts into knots.

But Chuck still held him there. Wouldn't let him fall even though all Kip wanted to do then was curl into a ball and weep.

He had forgotten all about Zak.

When his cousin's face suddenly appeared over Chuck's shoulder, it was like seeing Batman come to his rescue.

Zak's hand slammed down on the back of Chuck's neck, squeezed hard. Kip could tell Zak was squeezing hard because the grin stretching across Chuck's face flipped into a grimace, and Chuck released Kip and sent him crashing to the concrete.

Kip's knees slammed against the pavement, and he yelped, rolled around for a minute clutching them. That's when he noticed Cash and Jerrod. Chuck's minions rolled around and moaned in the street, neither one of them worried about Chuck anymore, too engulfed in their own pain to care.

Chuck spun in place, shrugging off Zak's hand. The jock threw a punch, and even Kip could tell it was sloppy.

Zak sidestepped it easily, actually smiled at Chuck as he put his fists up.

He really is like Batman.

Chuck studied his friends writhing in pain on the ground. Cash clutched his stomach, and Jerrod cupped his face with both hands and squealed like a stuck pig.

"You think you can take me, motherfucker?" Chuck spat on the street, cracked his knuckles. "I'm gonna fuck you up so bad, your face'll look worse than Toad's over here."

"Don't fucking call him that," Zak said as he rushed forward.

Chuck stood his ground, threw a couple of punches at the approaching boy. They weren't as sloppy as the last one, but neither of them landed true. His right fist brushed the side of Zak's head, but did nothing to slow him.

When Zak's fist slammed into the side of Chuck's face, Kip's skin reacted with an orgasmic burst of pleasure. Every inch of him pulsed now, and he smiled wide as he watched his cousin's fist hit home again, this time throwing Chuck off his feet.

Chuck rocked back and forth on the ground, eyes pinched tight, mouth bleeding. He growled, forced himself back to his feet. His eyes rolled toward Kip, and he spat a wad of red mucus into the street, breathing hard through his nose.

The other boys were getting to their feet too, and for a second, Kip thought they would surround Zak, jump him from every angle. And if they did, Kip didn't know if Zak could take them, not all at the same time.

And I'm the only one who could help him. Oh no...

But they didn't do that. Chuck's minions limped and dragged their sorry asses back to the Mustang. Chuck shot them a look, twisted his mouth in disgust. He turned back toward Kip, pointed a hard finger like a stick of dynamite.

"This shit ain't over, motherfucker. You hear me?"

Kip noticed that Chuck left the Toad part out. Kip smiled wider, and Chuck's face got redder.

Chuck turned toward Zak, looked about ready to say something, but then just stomped off, slammed his car door, and peeled out. The car tilted onto two wheels when it turned, and then was out of sight, though Kip could still hear the engine roaring in the distance.

"You okay?" Zak held out a hand, pulled Kip to his feet.

Kip reminded himself that he was mad at Zak, that he was

going to give him the silent treatment. *But that was before he kicked Chuck's ass. And Chuck's minions.*

"I didn't know you could fight like that," Kip said, unable to make himself stop grinning. "That. Was. Awesome."

"Thanks," Zak said, and dusted his hands. "All in a day's work."

"Where'd you learn to kick ass so hard?" The throbbing in his skin began to calm, and the euphoric sensation dissolved bit by bit. Made it easier for Kip to get his thoughts together. He couldn't wait to get home and pop some more of the zits though, especially the whopper on his bottom lip.

"I learned with you. All those super hero fights we use to have? You remember that?"

"Of course I do! You couldn't have learned how to fight from that. If that was the case, I'd be a bad ass. And...uh, I'm not."

Zak cackled, patted Kip on the back, then slid Kip's backpack off his back for him and tossed it into the Corolla. "Okay. Maybe I had to learn to defend myself when my mom's boyfriend decided it was fun to kick our asses all the time. But still...our battles helped."

Kip smiled, rubbed his shoulders where the backpack's straps had been digging in.

"I'm sorry about today. I promise I didn't mean for that to happen," Zak said.

They walked back to the car and Kip slid into the passenger seat. He faced Zak and shrugged. "I was kind of mad. But not anymore. Thanks for sticking up for me...and for telling that asshole to stop calling me Toad. I hate that name."

"Of course you hate that name. It's an awful thing to call someone. If that dickhead messes with you again, he won't get off so easy."

It's true. Things really are going to get better now that I have my cousin back. This is great!

"So...um..."

"Yeah? What's up?"

"Did you...you know. You and Jade. Did you skip class because you wanted to screw her?"

"Screw her? Really, cousin?"

Kip just shrugged, felt his zits start to move again, but he calmed himself down and just smiled.

"The plan was to take her to school, but she was… insistent. That girl is nothing but trouble, I'll just say that. I won't be seeing her again." Zak's brow lowered a bit and he shook his head slightly.

"You're breaking up with Jade? But she's so…she's got such big—"

"I know. Trust me, it's not worth the trouble. And it's not like we were a couple or anything…I just need to stay away from her. She's bad news for me."

"I guess. I can't imagine having the chance to be with her and passing up on it." But even as the words left his lips, it wasn't Jade's face he was seeing in his mind, but Gwendolyn's. That last look she had given him before walking out of the cafeteria, eyes slightly squinted, almost like she wanted to say something to him.

"You got a thing for Jade, cousin?"

"Doesn't everybody? I mean…look at her!"

"Oh I looked at her, all right. And I saw nothing but tits and crazy. You think her tits are big, you should see her crazy."

"But there's someone else." Kip smiled. "She's the only girl who's ever talked to me."

Zak punched Kip in the arm. "Oh yeah? Who is this?"

"It's not like you think. She talks to me because she feels sorry for me. That's all…but I don't care. She's perfect."

"I'm still waiting, cousin. Who is she?"

Kip almost said her name, but chewed it back down. "Just…somebody. That's all."

When they got back to Kip's house, they went straight toward Kip's room. He stood on his tiptoes and pulled the attic door down, pulled out the stairs.

"Nice fucking spread, man." Zak walked straight to Kip's bookshelf and started flipping through the comics. Every issue in a plastic sleeve with a cardboard back. Superhero and movie monster action figures stood atop the shelf, all lined up as if frozen in the middle of some epic mash up battle.

35

"Holy shit," Zak said. "You kept all your old comics from when we were kids?"

"Yep. Every one. I've got all my comic cards in binders too. All still in perfect condition."

"I'm having a nerdgasm over here. I haven't even thought about comic books since…well shit. Since I used to come over to your house and play."

The two of them spent the afternoon playing video games, going through comic books, and flipping through Kip's binders. It felt like old times, and Kip couldn't remember a time when he had felt happier.

"Hey, Kip?" Zak said.

Kip paused his game. "Yeah?"

"I'm sorry for lying to you, man. About going to class, you know? I've been feeling bad about it all day."

Kip rolled his eyes, unpaused the game. "Don't worry about it. You broke it off with Jade, right? So you won't have to miss anymore class. And don't forget…you got me if you need any help with your schoolwork. From what I hear, I'm kind of a genius."

Zak reached over and decked Kip in the shoulder. "Yeah yeah, rub the shit in."

Kip could hardly catch his breath. The controller slipped from his hand and he leaned back, let his body fall onto the carpet as the feeling spread from his shoulder all the way down his spine. There must have been a zit on the verge of bursting where Zak had hit him, and when Zak's fist collided with it, it popped, filled him with elation.

"Kip? What…what are you doing, man?"

Kip forced himself back to a sitting position, gripped his knees to calm the shaking. "N-nothing. I was just…just messing around."

"Okay," Zak said, one eyebrow higher than the other. "So…there's something I want to talk to you about. It's gonna sound bad, okay? Just…just trust me on this. And don't get all worked up either."

"Um…"

"Have you ever heard of Senior Skip Day?"

Even through the vibrating pleasure radiating up and down Kip's back, he was able to frown. "What are you talking about, Zak?"

"It's like a student holiday, man. Had the same thing back in California. Everyone does it, I'm telling you. It's not a big deal."

Kip just shook his head, was hoping Zak was just messing around.

"Come on, Kip. Everyone skips on this day. Everyone. Even the teachers know about it."

"Are you being serious right now? You just apologized for lying to me." Blood trickled down Kip's back, felt like a feather tip sliding down his skin. He wanted so bad to check the ruptured pimple in the mirror, finger the pus out.

"And that's why I'm telling you up front. There's a big party. From what I hear, all the...you know...cool kids will be there. I bet even your mysterious dream girl might be there." Zak reached over as if to nudge Kip again, but Kip avoided it. "I want you to come with me. This could be your chance to lose the Toad label, man. Break out of your cocoon...become a butterfly."

"A butterfly?"

"Okay, I don't know what the fuck I'm talking about. But seriously...I want you to come with me. It's one day. Teachers don't teach anything important on Senior Skip Day. I bet every one of them shows a video or some shit."

Gwendolyn wouldn't be caught dead at one of these parties. No way. But...but what if she was there? What if this is my big chance to talk to her? Really talk to her.

"I don't know. I don't think anyone is going to want me there. It'll ruin the party."

"Not if you're with me. And besides, they don't know you. Not like I do. They're just a bunch of stupid kids being mean...it's what they do. They can't help it, man."

"Right. It's basic instinct to make my life a living hell every single day. Is that what you're saying?"

Just then, Kip heard his mom's car pull into the driveway.

"I can't. I'm sorry, Zak. You go if you want…and I won't even get mad. I don't care, okay? But I can't."

Before Zak could say another word, Kip jumped to his feet and dashed toward the door. He always greeted his mom when she got home from work, and he meant to keep the tradition going. Well, that and he didn't want to hear his cousin try and persuade him to skip class anymore.

"Kip," Zak called out from behind him. "Come on, man."

Kip was already halfway down the stairs. Zak followed, worry distorting his face like he had a mouthful of spoiled milk.

"You won't…you know. You won't tell Aunt Jenny about any of this shit, right? Me skipping, or even the fight. She can't know. Please."

"Relax. I'm not going to say anything. I'm just going to say hi and give her a hug."

They walked down to the first floor together, Zak becoming more nervous-looking the closer they got to the front door.

"You're a real good kid, Kip. Seriously."

"Thanks. But it's not like I—"

The front door exploded open and Kip's mom stormed in. At first, Kip thought something was wrong, thought something had happened to her. His heart got to thumping and his skin got to boiling.

Thump…thump…thumpthumpthumpthump.

But then he saw the smile on her face. She dropped to her knees in front of Kip and immediately hugged him, squeezed him tight.

"Mom…what's going on?"

"Honey," she said, grabbing Kip by both shoulders. Her grip tightened over the wound where Zak had popped his zit, and he had to concentrate to keep his eyes from rolling. "They're sending me to New York. Can you believe it? Me! Out of everyone in the office, they chose me!"

She made a sound like *eeeeek* and then hugged Kip again.

"Wait…what do you mean? New York?"

"A business trip. To meet with a big client there. This is huge, Kip. Huge. This could mean bigger and better things for us, baby."

"You're leaving to New York, Mom? When?" He tried to hide the shakiness from his voice, but it was loud and clear.

His mom noticed it too, because she let go of him, stood up, straightened out her pant suit. "I leave on Monday. I'll be gone for a week. Kip...aren't you excited? You know how hard I've been working and—"

"Mom, of course I'm excited. But what am I going to do?"

Zak cleared his throat, and Kip shot him an ugly look.

"Honey, you're seventeen years old. I trust you. You are a smart boy and can take care of yourself. At least for a week you can." Then she turned her attention to Zak, and whatever smile she had been presenting hid behind her scowl. "And I expect you to behave yourself, Zak. If I find out any funny business went on here while I was gone..."

Zak held up both hands. "It won't be a problem. Kip and I will have a great time together. Just like we used to when we were kids. Right, Kip?"

Kip didn't answer, just crossed his arms and pouted his lips. He knew he was being childish but didn't care.

"Kip, honey..."

"It'll be like a weeklong sleepover, man. It'll be fun... you know. After our homework is done and everything." Zak shot a nervous smile at Kip's mom.

"I trust that the two of you will do just fine." She had her eyes on Kip, the wrinkles on her forehead deepening by the second. "Well...I was going to order pizza for dinner to celebrate. But I guess we can just—"

"I'm sorry, Mom. I'm happy for you, I really am. I guess I've just never been away from you for that long before." Kip commanded his mouth to smile, and though it fought back, it eventually gave in. "Let's order pizza. We *should* celebrate. I'm proud of you, Mom. I know you've been working your... a-ass off. You deserve it."

She chuckled, one hand on her hip. "Well okay! What

kind of pizza do you boys want? I'm going to crack open a bottle of wine, and I'll even let you boys have a glass each. A small glass."

"No thank you, ma'am," Zak said. "But maybe we could get some Sprite?"

She arched her mouth and nodded. "Okay, fine. Kip?"

"Sprite for me too. And can we get Hawaiian pizza?"

"Sprite and Hawaiian it is then!"

The pizza was damn good. For the first time since he'd gotten there, Zak was finally starting to feel comfortable. Starting to feel like he was part of the family.

He had to admit, it felt good to see his cousin. Ever since that asshole Ernie came into his and his mom's life, Kip hadn't even entered his mind. But being back at Aunt Jenny's house, it felt like old times. He really did feel like the kid that used to play superheroes and read comic books.

He felt wonderful.

Aunt Jenny was in the best mood he'd seen her in. She was actually kind of pretty when she was smiling and laughing. Zak could tell that Kip still didn't like the idea of her leaving out of town, but Zak couldn't help but see opportunity there. Not to throw a party or do anything stupid, but it was his chance to show Kip a really good time. Try and break the kid out of his shell a little, maybe even get him laid.

Though Zak had to admit that last part might be a little tricky.

Kip wasn't an ugly kid. Not really. Sure, his acne was awful, looked like red fungus growing all over his face and the back of his neck, but that would go away in time. It was his shyness he had to get over, and that was something Zak was sure he could help with.

He's coming to the Senior Skip Day party. Even if I have to club him over the head and carry him over my shoulder.

Zak knew that Chuck and his two jock buddies would be there. And he knew that they wouldn't let the fight go. Especially when they were fueled by alcohol. He would have to bring some protection just in case. The gun belonged to

Ernie, and Zak had swiped it just before heading to Aunt Jenny's. He didn't take it because he thought he would need it, but he didn't like knowing the gun was at home while he wasn't. He didn't trust that motherfucker with it.

He hoped he wouldn't have to flash it, but he would feel a lot better knowing it was there if he needed it.

"So," Zak said as he patted his belly and tossed the last chunk of pizza crust into the now empty box. "Kip said he'd tutor me. Isn't that right, Kip?"

"Yeah. Zak said he's really trying to do better, Mom. I believe him." Kip shot Zak a smile that would have screamed homo if it came from anyone else. Zak just smiled right back.

"Is that right?" Aunt Jenny reached over and patted Zak on the back of the head. Her face was a little pink from the bottle of wine she had polished off on her own. "I'm so glad to hear that."

Zak beamed, slugged Kip on the arm. His cousin got that faraway look in his eye again, almost like he was cumming in his pants. It was weird, gave Zak the creeps.

Is this kid some kind of closet pervert or something? When Aunt Jenny leaves, is he going to where her underwear and lipstick and dance around the house?

No. Zak knew that wasn't it. The kid was probably doing his best to hide how bad it hurt him whenever Zak playfully hit him. Kip was so skinny, Zak realized his knuckles were probably hitting bone.

After dinner, Zak and Kip headed back up to his room. Zak sat on the bed and frowned when Kip went right back to his video game.

"Hey, man. What about that movie? Are we still going?"

"Nah. Don't feel like it anymore."

"Come on, Kip. Are you really that upset that your mom's leaving? Most kids would be happy about that."

Kip shot Zak a side glance. "Well I'm not like most kids, remember? I'm the Toad. And I guess I'm just a fucking pussy because I don't want her to leave."

Whoa. Where the hell did that come from?

"Relax, man. It'll be great, just the two of us. We won't

throw a party or anything, don't worry. But maybe we can get some girls to—"

"Nope. Nobody's coming over to my house. Nobody. I'm not breaking a promise to my mom, okay?"

"All right, all right."

Zak decided not to press the matter too much. He was just about to bring up Senior Skip Day again, but knew the timing was bad. Let the kid sulk for a little while.

Zak lay on the floor, propped his head up on a folded pillow. He opened up a comic book, an old X-Men he remembered reading years ago. Before long, he was out.

CHAPTER FOUR

The weekend went by too quickly. Kip knew he was being ridiculous, but he didn't want his mom to leave. He also knew that Zak was right, that he should be excited about being at home without an adult, just him and his cousin. It seemed like the perfect set up too. They could invite some girls over, just like Zak had started to say the other night before Kip had cut him off. Zak didn't bring it up again, and for that Kip was grateful.

And even if we did invite some girls over here, they wouldn't do anything with me. They would be here for Zak.

His mom had left the house a couple of hours ago. She didn't know he was awake. They had said their goodbyes the night before, and Kip did everything he could not to show how upset he was. He just smiled at her, hugged her, told her how happy he was that she was getting this opportunity.

She just kept saying how good this was for them, how if things went right their lives would be so much better. But Kip didn't think they had a bad life. As far as he was concerned, everything at home was just how he liked it. It was the only place he felt safe, the only place he felt he belonged.

He couldn't sleep. Just knowing his mom was probably on an airplane right then, leaving him, he had tossed and turned for hours before finally giving up and just getting out of bed. Zak lay on his stomach, his breaths rattling as he slept. Kip almost woke him up, just to have someone to talk to, keep him company, but decided to leave his cousin alone.

He stood in the bathroom in front of the mirror, all of his clothes piled onto the floor. The acne looked like it was getting worse. Since he found out about his mom leaving for a week, his skin reacted with an explosion of new pimples, flowing over his entire torso like red lizard skin.

Each bump looked filled to capacity with milky white pus. The whiteheads gleamed in the fluorescent light of the bathroom, coated in a thin layer of grease.

As he stared at himself, the zits got to moving, pumping and thrusting. Waves of pulsating movement across his body like ripples. A couple of them burst from the rapid thrashing, squirting white and red gunk onto the sink and splattering across the mirror.

It felt so good, Kip was already stroking himself before he even realized what he was doing. He scraped his nails across his chest, bursting three of the larger zits like tiny water balloons. The pus squirted into the palm of his hand, and he used it as lubricant, biting his lip as the pleasure rode his flesh in rhythmic bursts.

It didn't take long for him to finish. He stared at his semen floating in the water of the toilet, looking like bleached man-o-war tentacles. After he flushed that down, he took another long look at himself. The pimples had calmed again, though the ones that had burst were now spewing a good amount of blood which mixed with his sweat and seemed to coat his entire chest and stomach.

He felt better. Turning his back to the mirror, he inspected the skin of his back and ass cheeks. The acne covered them, all sizes and stages of growth, the skin a neon red. Some of the zits were so big they looked like nipples with white tips and red areola. Kip tried to reach back and pop them, but couldn't reach. He got a few on his shoulders, and could have reached the ones on his lower back and ass, but decided to save them for later.

But that big bastard on his bottom lip still wasn't quite ready. No whitehead, just a big red bump, and every time he tried to squeeze it, it only made the thing bigger, more irritated. After going at it for about ten minutes and doing nothing but making it worse, Kip gave up, ran his tongue across the oiled mountain of red flesh.

The pills sat on the bathroom counter. A small paper box, a big picture of a pregnant lady with a red X slashed across her. There were even drawings of deformed babies, warning

Kip of how powerful the drugs were, that if a pregnant woman took them, there wasn't just a chance she could have birth defects, it was a goddamn certainty.

"Worthless pills," Kip whispered as he balled the package up and tossed it into the trash. There was no hope to cure his acne. He knew that now.

And the more he thought about it, he wasn't sure he wanted to cure it.

It was who he was. It defined him.

The acne might be the only good thing he had going for him.

Before walking out of the bathroom, he ran a loving hand over his face, his chest. The scabrous and oily flesh tickled his palm, and then he cut the light off and went back to his room.

Chuck busted a good nut, rubbed it over Jade's ass cheeks like lotion. Such a perfect ass. Nothing like seeing his own cum splash across it.

Jade, still bent over, clicked her tongue. "Get me a fucking towel. I hate when you do that shit."

"Chill out. Let me catch my fucking breath."

She rolled her eyes, swiped his shirt from the floorboard of his Mustang.

"Hold up, don't—"

But she was already sliding the fabric over the creamy mess, wiping it off, then threw the shirt into Chuck's face.

The wetness hit him right in the mouth, and he tossed the shirt away, spat, gagged. "What the fuck is your problem?"

"What's wrong? You got your nut off, didn't you?"

Chuck wanted to slam his fist into the back of her head, but she was right. Jade was easily the best piece of ass in school, and any time she was in the mood for some Chuck, he made sure to get his ass—and cock—there as quickly as he could. Before she changed her mind, which she was prone to do.

"I guess you're right about that, baby." He leaned over, kneaded her breasts, tweaked her dark nipples. It wasn't until he tried to kiss her that she stopped him, crammed her open palm into the middle of his face and shoved him away.

"We're done. Quit fucking touching me for a second, okay?" She pulled a joint out of her purse, lit it. "Can't find my fucking coke. Probably left it in Zak's car."

Chuck slammed his fist into the back of the driver's seat headrest. "I swear to god, if you bring up that motherfucker one more time, I'm kicking you the fuck outta this car."

Jade only smiled, let the dense smoke roll from between her fat, pink lips. Sweat beads covered her face and chest like clear pimples, bringing that little fucker Toad to Chuck's mind.

"What do you have against Zak? You just fucked his girl, didn't you?" She took a long draw from the joint, then finally passed it to Chuck. "What is it with you fucking jocks, man? Always gotta pick on people. What, he's the new guy, so you and your fucking lughead friends gotta give him shit?"

Chuck took a deep hit, blew the smoke right into her face. "I don't wanna talk about that cocksucker. Didn't I just tell you that? And what's this about you being his girl?"

She only shrugged, still waving the smoke out of her face. "Like I said. We might've had a little fight, but that don't mean anything."

"That fuckhead's been in town, what, a week? And you already claimed him, huh? Then why you here with my cum all over your ass?"

"Told you. We had a fight. I was horny. Is that a fucking problem?" She reached over and snatched the joint from his fingertips. "Where's your little cheerleader, Chuck? Shouldn't your dick be with her instead of me?"

Chuck's dick was now limp, stuck to the side of his inner thigh with Jade's fluids. He pulled his pants up, nearly pulled his shirt on before he remembered it was thick with his nut.

"I already told you. I'm done with that bitch. She's fucking annoying, man. Nags constantly." He scooted closer to Jade, grabbed the back of her neck. She tried to fight him off, but he wouldn't let her, pulled her in and kissed her long and hard. The smoke she'd been holding in burst into his mouth, but he didn't care. When he finally let her go, she slapped him, but had a small smile pulling at the corners of her mouth. "I love you. I don't love her. Never did. It's you I want."

Jade shook her head, started pulling her clothes back on. When she started laughing, Chuck nearly clocked her on the side of the head, but held back, concentrated on the bulge of her tits against her white t-shirt, the way her nipples pressed up against it like thick pencil erasers.

"You're joking, right?" she said.

"Whatta you mean?"

"Did you really just say that you love me? Because if you did, you better be fucking joking."

But I do love you. I've always loved you.

"Because I just got done telling you that me and Zak, we're a couple. I'm his girl. So keep your motherfucking love to yourself."

Chuck had so much he wanted to say right then, but he bit his tongue. He knew when to push Jade and when to back off, and by the tone of her voice, he knew which to do then.

"Take me home, man."

"No problem." Chuck didn't say another word to her all the way to her house. When they pulled up, Jade had the door open before he had ever pulled all the way over.

"See you." She eased the door shut and started walking toward the house.

"Wait," Chuck said, trying to whisper as loud as he could. "You going to the party?"

Without turning to face him, she just said. "I'll be there. With my man."

And then she entered the house and was gone.

Chuck smiled, checked his face in the rearview mirror. His chin was bruised some, but not as bad as he thought it would.

Yeah, you'll be with your man. And when I see that motherfucker, he'll wish he never moved here.

And then once he took care of Zak, once he got that asshole out of the picture completely, Toad was history.

He pulled his cell phone out of his pocket, dialed Chelsea's number.

47

It rang six times, and just when Chuck was going to give up…

"H-hello? Chuck?"

"Hey, baby. What you doing?"

"What time is it?"

"Does it matter? I wanna see you. Now."

There was silence, and then a soft giggle. "You're so bad. My parents are asleep. You can climb in through my window…just like last time."

"Good. Be there in ten."

CHAPTER FIVE

Kip attempted to cook eggs that morning, but he burned them. He tossed the yellow and brown mess into the sink, spun the disposal.

"You wanna run by the Grease Shack on the way to school today?" Kip said to Zak who was just walking in after smoking his morning cigarette. "I'll buy."

"Yeah, sure."

Kip woke up in a good mood. He expected to wake up depressed, missing his mother, but that wasn't it at all. He felt invigorated, full of energy.

He felt like a different person, a new man.

They ate breakfast tacos as they made their way to school, the cheesy eggs and sausage hitting the spot just right. Once they parked, Zak turned to face Kip.

"You know what tomorrow is, Kip?"

"Um...Tuesday?"

"No. Well yeah, but... It's Senior Skip Day. Look, I know what you're going to—"

"I'm in." Kip knew Zak was going to bring it back up eventually, and he had already decided to go along with it. It was time for a change. Besides, Kip knew that even if any of his teachers decided to spring a pop quiz or something that day, Kip could always tell them he was sick. Not a single one of them would have suspected him of skipping class, even on Senior Skip Day.

"Are you serious?" Zak had his hands together like he was praying, and his face was full of teeth as he grinned.

"Yeah, screw it. It's just one day, right? And besides... if Gw...if my girl is there like you say she might be, then it would be worth it. I'll talk to her, maybe ask her out or something." Even making that statement felt awkward, and

Kip knew that when it came down to it, if Gwendolyn was there, he probably wouldn't go through with it. In fact, he knew he wouldn't.

"That's what I'm talking about. Hell yes!" Zak looked ready to grab hold of Kip's shoulder, but he stopped, pulled his hand back. "You won't regret it, Kip. I promise. This is gonna be one hell of a party."

"Can I ask you something though?"

"Okay."

"What about Chuck? Don't you think he's gonna be there?"

Zak just smirked. "You leave that asshole to me. Don't even worry about it."

Kip just nodded. "What do you think about maybe going to that movie tonight? You know…since we didn't go Friday night?"

"Whatever you want, cousin. Sounds good."

The day went by fast, and with no incident. There was the usual name calling, some shoving, but nothing out of the ordinary for Kip. His heart nearly stopped and his skin nearly bubbled right off him when he saw Chuck walking down the hall toward him, but as they passed each other, Chuck didn't so much as glance his way.

Holy shit, is this really happening? Did Zak scare Chuck so bad that he won't even look at me anymore?

When the day was over, he met Zak back at the car. They made a quick stop back home, just to change clothes. Zak let Kip borrow a shirt since the only ones Kip owned all had either superheroes or movie monsters printed on them, and even though they were going to see a horror flick, Zak wouldn't let him wear one.

"You don't know who we'll see out there. What if your girl is there? Don't you wanna look good for her?"

Kip went along with it, even though he felt stupid. But the night went great. They didn't run into any girls, unless they counted the girl at the ticket counter who was overweight and looked like she had some kind of mental retardation.

Kip was glad though. He didn't really want to run into

Gwendolyn, or any girls from school. If that happened, Zak's attention would be on them instead of him. But the two of them were the only ones in the theater except for one guy sitting way in the corner.

The movie was great, even better on the big screen. Zak said he loved it—Kip knew he would. Plenty of blood and gore and naked boobies. What's not to love? They had shared a bucket of popcorn, drowning in liquid butter, and each had a box of Junior Mints.

Afterward, they stopped back at the Grease Shack for burgers and fries. Even though Kip wasn't hungry, he ordered some food anyway, nibbled at it absently. Zak finished his off, wiped his greasy hands over his thighs, then pulled out his pack of cigarettes.

"Can I have one of those?" Kip said. He balled up the half burger that was left and tossed it into the trash.

"What...a cigarette?" Zak laughed, but handed him one. Lit it for him. "You know how to smoke one of those?"

Kip didn't answer, just puffed on it, then started choking. He shook his head as he tried to catch his breath.

"Look," Zak said, and inhaled gently, the cherry glowing bright orange. He let the smoke flow out of his nostrils. "Don't suck on it so hard."

The cigarette tasted awful, but Kip kept taking small puffs, didn't choke again.

"Look at you, cousin. Really letting loose, huh? You were so upset when your mom left, I thought this week was gonna be a nightmare, you know?"

"I was upset. I don't know...she's the only friend I ever had. I've never been away from her for more than a day. But now that she's gone, it's like...I feel different."

"Different how?"

"I don't know. Just different. I want to try things. I'm sick of being...me. The Toad." Kip stared at his reflection in the side mirror. "Remember that episode of Seinfeld when George decided to do everything opposite of what he would normally do? And then everything starts going really well for him?"

51

"Um...no. Don't watch much TV these days."

"Oh. Well, that's what I want to do. Maybe things will get better if I do."

"Well, don't stop being you. Never stop being you, Kip. But that doesn't mean you can't have a little fun, right?"

"Yeah. I want to have some fun."

They finished their cigarettes, catching glances from the other kids coming and going from the Grease Shack. All kids from school. Kip could tell that most of them didn't know Kip and Zak were cousins, couldn't figure out why a guy like Zak would be hanging out with someone like Toad.

That's right. We're family. We're best friends.

Kip couldn't wait for tomorrow. It would be a new day. Tomorrow, he wouldn't be Toad. Things would be different from now on, he just knew it.

CHAPTER SIX

The first thing he noticed that morning was the size of the zit on his lip. It looked ready.

I can't go to the party with that thing on my face.

Even though the tip had turned white, and it shone like a teary eye, it still wouldn't give. Kip grunted in frustration as he squeezed, but the thing only became more irritated, made his lip puff up.

God, I look awful.

The pimples looked especially bad that morning. Had grown worse in the last 48 hours. Part of him wondered if he was having some kind of skin emergency, that maybe he should get Zak to drive him to the hospital or something. Some kind of side effect or allergic reaction to the pills. Every inch of his chest and back was covered in red fleshy bumps, most of them topped with a fat, glistening whitehead. It looked like if he so much as flexed, they would burst and spray pus and blood all over the place.

He pulled his boxer shorts down and stared at the massive bumps on his ass. He prodded them with his finger, sucked in a quick breath as tiny bursts of pleasure flashed across his skin.

The zits on his forehead, cheeks, chin, and nose all begged to be popped, but he left them alone. It was a battle he wouldn't win, and even if he popped each one, it wouldn't help his appearance. Trading white-tipped bumps for scabby open wounds.

Just don't think about it. Do like Zak said. Be confident. If Gwendolyn is at the party, show her that you're not scared.

"Yeah, right."

Knock, knock, knock.

"You jerking your dick in there, cousin? Hurry up, I gotta massive load to drop!"

"Okay okay." Kip gave himself another long look in the mirror before pulling a t-shirt over his head and slipping into his favorite jeans. When he opened the door, he was nearly trampled by Zak who didn't even wait for him to leave before dropping his pants and popping a squat right there on the toilet.

"Sorry, Kip. Emergency."

Kip shut the door as fast as he could so he wouldn't have to endure anymore, and just as the door clicked, Zak's voice rang out.

"And if you think you're going to the party wearing that, you're dead wrong. We're going shopping today, cousin."

Kip had been hoping Zak would let him borrow another shirt anyway. He wanted to look his best for Gwendolyn, though he still doubted she'd be there at all. He couldn't imagine her taking part in Senior Skip Day, but then again a day ago, he would have said the same thing about himself.

Just thinking about her sent tremors through his body, made his skin so sensitive that every movement, every step he took was ecstasy. He wanted nothing more than to hide away somewhere and pop each and every zit on his body. Better than jacking off. But he forced the thoughts from his mind, focused on preparing himself mentally for tonight.

Once Zak was finished, they both agreed to pick up some breakfast on their way to the store. It felt weird not going to school on a Tuesday. Felt wrong. Kip couldn't shake the panicky feeling swelling in his belly.

"You all right?" Zak asked through a mouthful of sausage biscuit.

"Huh? I'm…I'm fine." Kip had ordered a coffee, thought it would help calm him, but it only made him more nervous, more jittery.

"Come on. What's the matter?"

"This feels so…bad. I've never done anything like this before. And also…you know…"

"Nervous about tonight?"

Kip nodded, stuffed the rest of his hashbrown into his mouth.

"Don't forget what I told you, Kip. Be confident, okay? The look you've got on your face right now, the way your hands won't sit still, it looks nervous. Girls don't like nervous."

Kip lifted his hands in front of his face and glared at them as if it was the first time he'd ever seen them. "What do I do with my hands then?"

"I don't know, shove them in your pockets. Let them just hang at your sides. Just stop fidgeting so much. Shit, you're starting to make *me* nervous just watching you."

Kip crossed his arms, sort of leaned to the side. "How about this?"

"Better. You look relaxed which is good. What are you going to say to her when you see her?"

Kip hadn't put any thought into that at all. "Um, I don't know. I can ask her how she thinks she did on our History test, or—"

"No. You won't mention school at all. Ask her about herself. What kinds of things she likes to do, her favorite movie, band, food, whatever. Get her talking, man. Girls love talking. Don't talk about yourself until she asks, got it?"

Kip almost doubled over as his flesh got to pulsating again, the thrashing becoming more and more violent as his anxiety filled him like the pus in his zits.

"Zak...I don't think I can do this. It sounds too complicated, and I know I'll mess up. I know I'll make a fool out of myself. In front of anyone."

Zak hit him. Cocked his fist back and slugged Kip right in the arm. There was no acne on the spot of impact, and an explosion of pain erupted there on his bicep, and his arm hung limp from his shoulder.

"Ow! *What was that for!*"

"What do you think? Every time you try and puss out on me, I'm gonna hit you again. Same spot every time."

Throb...throb...throb.

Zak tilted his head, squinted as he stared at Kip's face.

Kip quickly turned away from him. "What?"

"Your...your face. I swear to god I just saw it moving. The pimples were like... beating."

"Oh, real nice, Zak. Like I'm not self-conscious about them enough already?"

"I was looking right at you, Kip. They moved, I'm serious."

Kip kept his head turned, willed his flesh to calm, to relax. After a few minutes it did, and he turned back to face his cousin. "You're seeing things."

"Oh yeah? Then why wouldn't you look at me?"

"Because I'm embarrassed, okay! I know how awful my skin looks, and seeing you staring at it like that kind of made me feel like a freak."

Kip, of course, knew Zak was telling the truth. But he didn't know what to say. He didn't know why his skin acted the way it did, knew it wasn't normal for acne to pulsate like that. His acne was different, special. *Super human.*

"You're right, man. I'm sorry. Didn't mean anything by it."

Kip waved it off. "Don't worry about it. I'm the Toad, remember? I'm used to people staring and laughing at me."

"Does…does it hurt? It looks really painful."

"Nah. Not really. I can hardly tell it's there until I look in the mirror. Or, you know, when people stare. But it doesn't bother me too bad."

"Well, I'll get you some clothes that are so sharp, nobody will even notice the zits. Bet on that."

"Okay. Yeah…that sounds good."

They went straight to the mall then, and Kip spotted a lot of students there from their high school. All enjoying Senior Skip Day. Kip couldn't help but wonder if anyone at all showed up to class, if the hallways were empty. He imagined tumble weeds blowing through the halls, teachers looking lost and confused.

Zak dragged Kip into a few different stores, Kip feeling uncomfortable and out of place in every single one of them. Every shirt, every pair of jeans Zak picked out, Kip shook his head.

"I'll look stupid in that."

Zak had clearly been doing his best to remain patient, but now he looked exhausted. He massaged his temples, spoke with his eyes closed. "Kip…cousin. The point is you want to try something different, right? Different means it might feel uncomfortable at first. But you gotta trust me. I'm picking something…right now…and you don't have a choice, understand?"

Kip tried to protest, but just lowered his head and nodded. Zak was trying to do something nice for him, he knew that. But he couldn't help but feel like a complete idiot. He just knew he would be the laughing stock of the entire party when he walked in wearing a button down shirt and khaki slacks.

You're going to be the laughing stock of the party no matter what you wear, Toad.

"Here," Zak said, forcing a smile as he thrust the new clothes into Kip's arms. "Go try this on."

"All right."

Kip had to admit, the clothes looked pretty damn good once he had them on. Not nearly as bad as he had thought. And he didn't look as skinny in that shirt, couldn't see his pimples poking out like hard nipples all over his torso.

When Gwendolyn sees me in this, she'll freak. She'll notice me for sure.

Kip was suddenly overcome with excitement for the party to start. He knew the other kids would give him a hard time at first, even with Zak there with him, but he didn't care. Before the night was over, they would accept him. They wouldn't outcast him anymore, wouldn't spend so much energy making sure he was miserable every single day of the week.

Kip stepped out, trying not to grin too hard.

Zak whistled. "Damn, cousin. If I was a chick, I'd totally fuck you and have your babies."

"Shut up. Does it really look okay?" Kip turned his hips, held out his arms.

"Looks great, man. How do you feel?"

"I feel pretty damn good actually. I'm kind of getting excited."

"That's what I'm talking about, cousin. Yes! You'll never forget this night, I promise."

Kip hoped he was right.

***

"I wanna see you again." Chuck paced back and forth in front of Jade's house. Her dad's car was in the driveway, but he didn't give a shit.

"Well that's too bad. I'm getting ready for the party right now."

"We've still got over an hour before it starts. Can't we spend some time together first? Come on, Jade. Don't fuck with me like this."

"Call your girlfriend, asshole."

Click.

"Shit!" Chuck slammed his fist into his chest, stared up at Jade's bedroom window. Her shadow moved back and forth behind the drape, and even from that distance, he could see the shape of her body. God, he wanted her so bad.

He knew his night was going to be filled with Chelsea's babble, her and all her cheerleader friends. And when they got drunk it was even worse.

It was Jade he wanted. Yes, he wanted to fuck her. He never wanted to stop fucking her. But he wanted more than that. He wanted her all to himself. And as soon as she said he could have her, he would break it off with Chelsea so damn fast...

Fuck.

"What's the deal, Chuck? Can we get goin' or what?" Jerrod said, fixing his hair as he stared into the side mirror.

"Yeah, come on. How long we gonna sit out here. She ain't comin' out, man. And who gives a fuck. There'll be plenty of pussy at the party." Cash ignited his lighter and touched the flame down onto the bowl he'd been smoking. He offered the glass pipe to Chuck.

Chuck took a hit, held in the smoke as he glared up at Jade's window. He blew it out, handed the pipe back to Cash. "Y'all shut the fuck up. We'll stay out here all fucking night if I say so."

Neither one of them talked back, but they smacked their lips, clicked their tongues.

"Fuck it. You're right. We can have our pick of the ass tonight. Right, fellas?" Chuck slapped hands with both of his friends as they agreed. "Fuck this bitch. I'm sick of her shit."

As they drove away, Chuck let Jade dissolve from his mind. Chelsea too.

It was Zak and Toad that filled his thoughts now. They were all he'd been thinking about for days. He dreamed about them, jerked his dick while he imagined stomping their fucking heads in.

And tonight, he would show Jade who the real man was. He would show Jade that she picked the wrong dude.

You're mine, bitch. He can't have you. Nobody can.

CHAPTER SIX

"What'd you bring that for?" Kip had opened the glove compartment when Zak told him he had a pack of gum in there. As soon as it was open, Kip could tell Zak had forgotten about the gun.

"You weren't supposed to see that."

"But why did you bring it?" Kip knew it was for Chuck before Zak said it. His cousin couldn't even look him in the eye. "So when you told me not to worry about Chuck and his friends…this is what you meant? That if he messes with us, you'll what? Kill them all?"

"No!" Zak's face was red and his knuckles white as he squeezed the gray steering wheel in his fists. "It's just to scare them. And it's only a precaution. If they don't fuck with me, with us, there won't be a problem."

"We should leave. This was a bad idea." Kip rocked in the car seat, staring out the window as the other kids filed into the house. Kip didn't even know whose house this was, but he recognized all the kids. The "cool kids," the same kids that were the worst to him every single day.

And now I'm here to, what, hang out with them? Who am I kidding?

"Don't blow this out of proportion, Kip. I'm not going to hurt anyone."

"Oh yeah? So say Chuck and his friends start something. And you pull your gun out. But they don't stop. Then what? You going to murder them in front of all the jocks and cheerleaders?"

Zak didn't answer, just stared blankly out the windshield.

They stayed silent, only the sound of their breathing and the tiny voice on the radio.

"I won't bring it inside, okay? You're right. It was a bad

idea."

"Zak, maybe we should just leave. Seriously. You don't know Chuck like I do. There's no way he's going to just let that fight go. No way in hell. Him and his buddies have probably been devising a plan to get us back since it happened."

Zak only smiled, pulled his Camels from his pocket, lit one. He offered one to Kip but Kip refused.

"That asshole is not gonna ruin our time. No way."

"Zak—"

"I'm not kidding. I learned a long time ago that the only way to make someone stop fucking with you is to show them you're not scared. We run now, Kip, and we'll always be running. I know that sounds fucking corny, but it's true. You're sick of being the Toad? Show this motherfucker you are. Show all of them."

Throb...throb...throb...

Kip couldn't help but be scared, but the pulsating euphoria began to ease his mind, and his cousin's words started to make more and more sense. A low moan escaped his lips, and even when Zak raised an eyebrow at him, Kip just smiled, ran his hand across his chest and let his eyes roll.

"Kip?"

"You're right. Let's go."

Zak slapped the steering wheel so hard, the horn honked. Some of the kids walking into the house turned to look, a few of them noticing that their class Toad had come to their precious party. Some of them frowned, but most smiled, knowing that if Kip was there, they would have plenty of entertainment for the night. They could all get drunk and make fun of him.

Not tonight. Not ever again.

Zak didn't really know any of the students from Bowie High. Mostly the girls. He'd never had a problem with the opposite sex, and as soon as he stepped foot on campus, they took notice. Jade pretty much claimed him right off the bat, and Zak went along with it purely off her looks.

It was the same back home at his high school. The girls

loved him, the boys wanted to hang out with him because, well, the girls loved him. So he never had a problem making friends. He could tell the same thing was happening now, and he hoped to use it somehow to help his cousin.

As they walked toward the house, Zak could feel the anxiety radiating off Kip like heat waves. The poor kid could barely look up, looked on the verge of having a panic attack. The other kids stared, and even though Kip said he was used to it, that it didn't bother him, it was already pissing Zak off.

"Hey, ladies," Zak said to a small congregation of girls, all sipping from red plastic cups. They giggled, faces turning pink, but when they saw Kip, their smiles faded away and were replaced with revulsion.

"What's he doing here?" one of the girls said, her eyes riding Kip's new clothes.

"He's my cousin, and he's with me. Is there a problem?" Zak placed his hand on Kip's shoulder, could actually feel the zits under the shirt.

The girls' eyes widened, and Zak could see a change in their attitude right away. They weren't jumping Kip's bones, but there was something different in the way they looked at him. As if he was just slightly less disgusting to them.

"Hi," Kip said.

The girls bust out laughing, turned their backs to him.

Or maybe not.

"Well, you bridge trolls have a good night. Let's go inside, Kip." Zak smiled as the girls gasped, mouths hanging open.

Kip snickered, looked over his shoulder at the group of girls. They were pretty, but Zak wasn't there to pick up girls. Not tonight. Tonight was all about Kip, and Zak wasn't sure how he'd pull it off, but he was determined to get his cousin laid. At the very least, a phone number.

As soon as they stepped into the house, music blasting, kids all shouting to be heard over the beat, all eyes turned on them. Conversations were cut off on a dime, and they all stared, whispering to each other, wrinkling their noses.

Zak thought for sure Kip would drop his head again, maybe wander off to a corner where he could hide, but he just smiled, waved at them all. Nobody waved back. Their eyes darted back and forth between Zak and Kip, clearly confused as to what was happening.

"Don't sweat this shit, Kip. Let them stare, they'll get over it."

"It's fine. I expected this, expected worse actually."

Zak didn't know how it could be any worse really. If he was in Kip's shoes, he didn't know how he would handle it. Would probably be suicidal or something. But Kip just smiled at them all as they stared, not a single one of them trying to hide their disgust.

Zak wanted to flip them all the double bird, but figured it would do more bad than good. Zak would have to take this slow.

Then he saw her. Jade already had her eyes on him, and she stood across the room with her two slutty friends, surrounded by guys. Each one of them rattled off their lines, doing their best to impress her, but she didn't appear to be hearing them at all. She had eyes only for Zak.

"Hey, cousin. Why don't you see about scoring us some drinks? Probably in the kitchen."

"Okay. Um…what kind?"

"A soda or something for me. You should have a beer."

Kip looked ready to refuse, but nodded instead. "Yeah okay. A beer…yeah."

Kip trotted off, all heads turning to watch him go. Jade was already on her way toward Zak leaving her group of hopefuls behind, all of them watching her go with either longing or anger in their eyes. Even her girlfriends looked annoyed.

She looked fucking great. A tight, black dress that showed every curve, cut low to display her perfect cleavage. As she weaved her way through the living room, every male in the place noticed. Every female did too, only they eyed her up and down with disgust contorting their faces.

"Hey. You didn't call." She leaned in for a kiss, and Zak kissed back, but only because he didn't know how else to react. She hugged him, wrapped her arms around his waist, slid her fingertips into his back pockets. "I missed you."

Zak wanted to shove the crazy bitch away from him, but didn't want to make a scene. And he knew this girl could cause one hell of a scene if she wanted to.

"I thought you were pissed at me," he said. "You sure as hell acted like you were."

She kissed his neck, writhed against him slightly. "So what if I was? Just because we had an argument doesn't mean anything. I still missed you. Where's your car?"

"What?"

"Your car. Where is it? We should leave. This party is fucking boring. I'd rather be alone with you anyway."

Now Zak did push her away, but gently. "Look, Jade. I told you before and I meant it, okay? I can't see you anymore. Not in that way."

"That's bullshit. Who could you possibly be fucking that's better than me, huh? You know I can have any fucking guy I want, right?"

She sounded like a child.

"I'm not stopping you. Take your pick."

She bared her teeth, and Zak braced himself for the onslaught. He figured he might as well get it over with. Maybe she would storm out afterward and then he and Kip could work on having a good time.

Before she could even start, Kip returned with their drinks. He handed Zak a bottled water, a cranberry wine cooler in his other hand. "They didn't have any soda. And I found this in there. Says here on the label it's got more alcohol than a beer…and I bet it tastes a lot better too."

"Thanks, cousin."

Jade spun around to face Kip, tried to press her ass against Zak's groin, but he backed away. He had never seen a girl be so aggressive before.

When Kip locked eyes with Jade, he visibly flinched, eyes widened. He smiled at her, but his eyes coasted toward the floor by his feet. Zak didn't blame him for this one—Jade was one intimidating bitch.

"Toad? What the fuck're you doing here?"

"He's here with me, Jade. And I told you I don't like that nickname."

She looked over her shoulder, bit her lip, raised an eyebrow. "Oh you don't? Did I hurt Toad's little feelings?"

"N-no. No you didn't. It's...um...it's totally fine." Kip hopped from foot to foot as if he was about to piss himself, then seemed to realize it and stood stock still. He took a drink of his wine cooler, made a face like he'd just taken a spoonful of cough syrup.

"You say I should take my pick, Zak? What if I pick your cousin, huh?"

When Jade stepped into Kip, wrapped her arm around his neck, Zak didn't know what was more amusing: the look on Kip's face or the look on everyone else's face.

Jade pulled Kip's drink out of his hand, slammed it in a couple of seconds. She placed the empty bottle back in Kip's hand, then she ran her fingers over his chest, the other combing through his hair.

"What do you think, Zak? Did I make a good choice?"

Zak tried to hold back his smile, but couldn't possibly. Kip looked like he was in the clutches of a grizzly bear, his eyes wide, slightly rolling as Jade ran her nails over his scalp, caressed his chest. Kip locked eyes with Zak for a split second, but then they coasted back to Jade's cleavage, which was pressed right up against him.

Zak figured this was probably the greatest moment in Kip's life, and he felt bad because he knew Jade was only doing it to try and get a rise out of Zak. It was only a matter of seconds before she did something to humiliate Kip, and Zak was trying to figure out some way to intervene, to stop it from happening.

Not a single person spoke. Even the music had been turned down a few notches. All eyes and ears were on the hottest girl in school and the Toad.

"I think you made a great choice," Zak said. "What do you think, Kip?"

Before Kip could answer, before he could even open his mouth, Jade slammed her face into his, locked lips with him.

Kip dropped the bottle and it shattered on the floor. And then Jade shoved him away screaming.

Kip had been concentrating on keep his erection at bay. Jade had her breasts mashed against his chest, and from where Kip was standing, he could see right down in between them, could see the peach fuzz on her belly. A scent rolled off of her like raspberries. The fingers running through his hair and against his scalp felt good. But it was her hand rubbing his chest that was creating the issue in his pants. The acne there sizzled with passion.

Though it was obvious she was only doing this to try and make Zak jealous, Kip didn't care. He'd take anything he could get. And having Jade Brewster press up against him like this, something he would have never thought possible in a million years, was like a dream.

He didn't see Gwendolyn there, and had been filled to the brim with disappointment, but this attention from Jade was helping him get over that pretty quickly.

And then the next thing he knew, she was kissing him. As her soft lips pressed up against his, he thought at first it was his imagination. That there was no way in hell this was really happening. Sure, rubbing up against him was one thing, but no girl, especially not Jade, would ever kiss the Toad. Kip couldn't believe it.

But there she was, face to face with him, lips puckered. They tasted like cherry lip balm. Kip didn't know he had dropped the bottle until he heard it crash, and in that same instant, something on his lip burst.

His face pulsated with intense pleasure at that moment, radiating out from the massive zit that had been giving him so much trouble for the past week. And it was Jade's mouth that finally did the thing in.

When Jade screamed and shoved away from him, he was still riding the euphoric spasms in his lip, riding his face like static. Then he saw the white glob smeared across her mouth.

Blood trickled down from the open wound on his lip, dripped onto the floor between his feet. Kip wiped it, stared at the amount of blood on his palm. Too much. He wondered if he should be worried, wondered how one zit could bleed so badly, but all he could do was smile, rub his fingers through it until it became sticky.

Jade's bottom lip quivered as she gagged. Then someone pointed at her face, followed by the gasps and laughter and the collective, "Ewwwwwww!"

"You've got pus on your mouth," one girl said.

Jade wiped it away, dropped to her ass as she stared at the thick white paste in her hand.

Oh god...it got in her mouth.

Kip was ready to leave now. Ready to go home where it was safe and crawl under his bed and never come out again. Nothing could have been worse than this. Even though his flesh still tickled and he still found it difficult to stop grinning, he shot Zak a quick glance that said, "Let's get the hell out of here."

Zak had the same flabbergasted look as all the others. His attention was fully on Jade, a sneer hooking the corner of his mouth.

But then Zak's expression changed. Right before Kip's eyes. It went from shocked amusement to just pure shock. Zak still had his eyes on Jade, so Kip let his gaze coast back to the girl on the floor in front of him.

Jade now had her eyes closed, bottom lip clamped between her teeth. She ran her hands across her body like she was smothering herself with invisible lotion. As her fingertips raced across the fabric of her tight dress, she breathed in quick gasps, as if her skin had become so sensitive that to touch it nearly brought her to orgasm.

What's happening?

Jade's eyes burst open—pupils dilated—and they burned a hole right through Kip's face. She was oblivious to all the others in the room with them, all the whispering and snickering. And then she was on her feet.

Kip thought for sure this was some kind of joke, that she was about to do something to embarrass him. Revenge for squirting a tablespoon's worth of pus into her mouth, coating her tongue and gums with it like melted plaque.

But it was pure ecstasy etched onto her face, and she stepped forward and slapped her lips against Kip's again, this time reaching around and cupping both ass cheeks with her hands. A few of the pimples on his backside popped, and he whimpered into her mouth.

Kip barely heard the collective gasp from all the others as Jade's tongue slithered into his mouth and spun like a helicopter blade. She moaned as she kissed him, swirled her hips. Kip didn't know what to do with his hands, and they both stuck straight in the air, palms out, as if holding them up for a police officer.

Jade pulled away from him with a loud smacking sound, darting her tongue out one more time and running it across the nest of zits on his chin. Her eyes were half closed, nipples fully erect.

She grabbed Kip's hands, pressed them up against her breasts, slid that tongue of hers across her lips as if licking up the remnants of whatever pus had been there before.

"More," she said, her voice low and whispery. "Give me more, Kip."

Kip could barely breathe as Jade pressed down on his hands, smashing them into her tits. He wanted to squeeze, but he couldn't make his fingers move.

"I...I..."

"So good... *So fucking good.*" And then she bit his chin. Clamped her teeth over the zits there, popped them all at the same time. The pus erupted into her mouth, and she rolled her tongue around in the white substance like it was melted ice cream, her lips tinged red with his blood.

Jade's knees went weak, and Kip thrust his arms out to make sure she didn't fall. She gasped, sucked in a lungful of air when Kip grabbed her. The rest of the kids in the house still watched, not sure what they were seeing, nobody making a sound. All just staring, mouths hanging open, eyes wide.

Kip finally looked toward his cousin. Zak stared right at him, his forehead a nest of wrinkles, his head shaking slightly from left to right. It looked like he wanted to say something, but he remained just as silent as all the rest.

Blood dripped from Kip's chin, and he wiped at it, but could do nothing to slow its flow. But he didn't care. His flesh was too enraptured for him to care. Every centimeter of his face swirled with delight, and he reached up to his forehead, squeezed one of the larger pimples with his thumb and forefinger until it burst, then held out the glob of pus for Jade like a priest offering a wafer.

This time, she widened her nostril, pressed the other one shut with her fingertip, and snorted the white mound into her nose. She instantly threw her head back, eyes squeezed shut, grunting. Her hands squeezed her breasts, violently, looked like she was trying to tear them free from her chest.

It felt to Kip like he was cumming out of his face. The blood dripped down into his eye, turned the room slightly red for a moment before he wrapped his arm around Jade's waist, pulled her in, and kissed her deeply. He didn't think about it, didn't have to, just reached out and claimed what was his. And he knew she wouldn't resist, knew she wanted him… needed him.

Jade's clique stepped up then, eyeing Kip like he was some kind of mythical creature. They looked scared to approach him, but they clearly wanted to get their friend away from him, as if he had done something to her to make her act this way.

The pus. The pus is doing this to her.

When the three girls tried to pull her away, she fought them off, clung to Kip's shirt like a cat avoiding bathwater.

"No…*no!* Get away from me."

"Jade…what's wrong with you?" Jezebel tried to grab Jade by the elbow, but was shoved off.

"What the fuck did you do?" Sasha said, jabbing a finger into the middle of Kip's chest. "You put some shit in your drink, man? What did you do to her?"

"I…I didn't do anything." Kip's eyes kept trying to roll as more waves of pleasure rolled over his face. "She did it. I don't—"

Sasha's face slammed against Kip's then. A zit on the side

of his face, right on his sideburn, ruptured, spat its custardy contents over Sasha's cheek. She squealed, shoved away, and it was then that Kip saw that it was Jade who had shoved her friend into Kip.

"You fucking crazy, bitch! His...his fucking pus got on me!"

Jade grabbed Sasha by the hair, pulled her head back as if she were trying to snap it off. Sasha yelped, mouth wide in pain. Jade's finger slid across the bloody pus on Sasha's cheek, and she popped the finger into Sasha's mouth, rubbed it hard across her teeth and gums, then let her friend fall backward onto the floor.

"Kip!"

Zak's voice.

In all the excitement, Kip had forgotten about his cousin. Zak weaved his way around the kids, who all seemed to be slowly making their way closer to the Kip.

"Kip...what's going on? What the fuck's happening?"

"Oh...*oh my god...*" Sasha squirmed on the ground, legs kicking, hands exploring her body as if feeling it for the first time. She inhaled sharply, then sat up, eyes wide and trained right on Kip. "Kip...oh my god."

Jade pulled Sasha to her feet, gripped her by the back of the neck, and pulled her close. Their tongues wrapped around each other, thrashing in the small space between their mouths.

Kip's knees went weak as his face thumped with pleasure, and just as he hit the ground, Jezebel dove on top of him. It was as if she couldn't take her two friends leaving her out, and she slid her tongue over Kip's face, drinking in the grease, finally pressing hard enough to pop another pimple. The pus was eaten up quick, and it didn't take long for the high to take effect.

The girls lay on the ground just in front of him, wrestled with each other. Licking and touching and rubbing, all of them with their eyes on Kip, staring deeply into him, pupils the size of pinpricks. He wanted to join them, to dive into their flesh and let them suck his skin dry, slurp up every ounce of pus in him like a human milkshake.

And then hands were on him from behind, lifting him, pulling him away from his girls. The girls reached for him, Jade now with her breasts free of her dress, begging Kip to come back to her, and he wanted to. He never wanted anything so bad.

"Kip, we need to leave. We need to go right now."

"No," Kip said, trying to fight off the hands gripping him hard on the arms, but he wasn't strong enough. "They want me. Don't you see? They need me!"

"Kip, fucking stop. We need to *go!*"

Kip was hauled to his feet, and it was then he noticed all the others. Reaching for him. Calling to him.

"Give me some, Kip. Come on, man!"

"I want to try. *Let me try!*"

"Don't hold out on us, Kip."

And Kip wanted to give it to them. He wanted to give it to all of them, boy or girl. It didn't matter anymore. The only thing that mattered was that he was wanted, he was desired. After seeing what his pus could do, the trio of girls now almost fully nude and wrestling on the floor, every kid wanted a taste of the Toad.

You can taste me. You can all taste me.

At first, Zak thought it was hilarious when Jade started to kiss Kip. Even when she started freaking out and shoved him away. Sure, Kip might get embarrassed, but he kissed a girl. And not just any girl, but Jade, a girl way out of his league. Zak knew Kip had probably been jerking his dick to Jade fantasies for years, and now he was locking lips with her.

That's my cousin!

But when she started touching herself, when she got that look on her face, Zak knew something wasn't right. She was fucked up on something, bath salts or some shit. She looked dangerous, hungry, violent.

Zak's muscles tensed up when she flung herself at Kip again, dragged her teeth across his chin.

Did she just fucking bite him?

He had been all set to jump in, get his cousin the fuck out

71

of there, but Kip had an expression like he had just busted a nut, and he wiped the blood off his chin and stared at it with a smile on his face.

What the fuck was in that drink?

Zak found himself cemented to his spot as the other girls joined in, and he watched along with everyone else as they started ripping each other's clothes off and rolling around on the floor together.

But then all the other kids got that hungry look, started to close in on Kip. It was as if they realized that there was something in Kip, something in his skin that was affecting these girls. Making them act like they'd just taken the strongest hit of ecstasy in the history of drugs.

His acne? They were sucking out the pus...oh god...

Even Zak started to feel weird, feeling the old need creeping up on him. He felt like he'd been up all night doing fat rails and had just run out of powder. That antsy, can't-sit-still feeling. That I-would-fucking-do-anything-for-just-one-more-hit feeling. It was as if Kip's flesh was spewing pheromones into the air or something, driving everyone in the room crazy. Plus, the trio of girls worked at each other, undulating and moaning. Kissing and sucking and fingering. Eyes all for Kip, soaked and dripping with passion.

We need to leave right now.

Zak didn't know how to explain what the fuck was happening, but he would think that over later. At the moment, he knew he needed to get him and his cousin the hell out of there, and quickly before the "cool kids" tore Kip apart to get at his candy center.

When Zak put his hands on Kip, he nearly lowered his face to the back of the kid's neck and sucked the pus out of the massive bush of zits there, their white tips looking like ripe fruit ready to burst, shining with oil, throbbing, surrounded by pink and red. He wanted to suck that pus right out, feel it melt over his tongue like butter, feel it ooze down his throat.

No. What the fuck is wrong with me?

Kip fought him, didn't want to leave. The kid didn't sound like himself, was entranced by their classmates calling his name, begging for a hit.

"Kip, fucking stop. We need to *go!*"

Zak managed to drag his cousin away from the girls, away from the outstretched hands, the horde of students like zombies straight out of a Romero flick. Only instead of brains and flesh, they craved pus and oil.

Even as Kip flailed, did everything in his power to break free of Zak's grip and run to the kids calling his name, Zak nearly had them out the door. Kip's arms and elbows kept slamming into Zak's face and neck, and Kip's heels collided with Zak's shins again and again. The door was right behind them, and Zak reached out for it, but before he could wrap his fingers around the knob, it flew open, nearly slammed into him but he dodged it at the last second. The door hit the stopper spring, made a *boing* sound, and then Chuck walked in, eyed glazed over, face red.

"Well well. Just the motherfucker I wanted to see."

The other two jocks strolled in behind Chuck, the same two knuckleheads he sucker punched. Even though he was able to take them before, he knew it was only because he had surprised them, clocked them from behind. Now, he wasn't so sure. Not only that, but there were other jocks at the party, and Zak was almost positive they'd back up Chuck.

"I'm gonna f-fuck you both up, you hear me? You're both fucking de..."

Chuck couldn't even finish his sentence as his eyes landed on Jade and her two friends, all three of them topless now, all three of them in the middle of pleasuring and being pleasured. And not a single person in that house cared. Nobody watched them, except for Zak, Chuck, and his buddies.

All eyes were still on Kip. Smothering him with aching want.

"What the fuck is going on!" Chuck forced his way past Zak and headed straight for Jade. "Put your fucking clothes on!"

She didn't even acknowledge him. Just kept licking, moaning.

"Chuck?" It was the cheerleader's voice. Zak couldn't

remember her name, but he knew it was Chuck's girlfriend. She'd been begging Kip for a hit only minutes before.

Jade finally untangled herself from her friends, did nothing to hide her nudity as she strolled across the room.

Zak tried to rush out the door, but the two jocks stood in his way, both scowling at him, clearly drunk out of their skulls.

Before Zak could stop him, Kip slipped free, sped toward Jade and met her halfway across the room. They locked mouths again, Kip reaching down and cupping her ass as she ran her tongue over his face.

"Somebody tell me what the fuck is going on!" Chuck screamed as his fist smashed through the wall.

"Chuck?"

Oh shit.

When Chuck had gone to visit Chelsea the other night, he thought he had convinced her not to show up at the party. Told her that he wasn't going to go either, that he had some things to do that night anyway, would meet up with her afterward.

And when he saw her standing there with her cheerleader friends, he could have smacked her. This was supposed to be his night with Jade, not her. And now Jade was on the ground, fucking naked and lesing out with her two ugly ass friends.

Chuck fought off the jealousy coursing through him, held back the urge to grab Jade, cover her up, and run out the door with her. He walked around the girls and straight for Chelsea.

"Chelsea…what are you doing here?"

He expected her to argue with him, ask him something like, "I thought you said you weren't coming!" but instead she hugged him, had a strange, stoned look in her eye.

There was a potent smell in the air, something that Chuck didn't recognize, but found very pleasant. He wanted to find the source of the smell and consume it, drown in it. The feeling came over him suddenly, and before he had to ask, Chelsea pointed a quivering finger. Toward Toad.

"It's him," she said. "You have to get some for us. Get as much as you can, okay? Hurry! I want it now, Chuck…*now!*"

"You what? I don't…I d-don't understand…"

"In his skin. Ungh…move!" Chelsea had given up on Chuck and was trying to force her way through the crowd, but it looked like everyone wanted the same thing.

Everyone wanted Toad.

And that's when Chuck saw Jade walking across the room. When she started kissing the Toad, sliding her tongue across his greasy face, Chuck couldn't take it anymore, didn't care if Chelsea found out about him and Jade.

His fist flew from his side and punctured the wall. White sheet rock dust drifted to the floor. Chuck's eyes were locked on Toad, but the little fucker wasn't paying him any attention, had his hands on Jade's ass, squeezing.

"Somebody tell me what the fuck is going on!"

A few heads turned his way, but only for a second. They all watched Toad. Watched as Jade used her teeth to pop a zit on his cheek and lick up the gravy.

Then the others started in. One at a time they stepped up to Toad, chose a zit, popped it, sucked up its contents. And they fucking loved it. Looked on the verge of orgasm, eyes rolling back, fists clenched, teeth bared, moaning… everybody moaning and whimpering.

Chuck lost Jade in the crowd, and he started muscling his way through, ready to rip Toad's acne-covered face right off his skull.

Then Chelsea was there, her mouth pressed up to Toad's neck, drinking in the pus and oil.

"Motherfucker!"

Chuck lowered his shoulder and surged through the mob. Bodies were slammed into each other, some hitting the floor. Chuck didn't slow his pace, kept shoving and punching until he had the little twerp right in front of him. There was a guy there now, had Kip's shirt pulled down at the collar. Shawn. The starting point guard on the basketball team. Shawn used his thumbnails to rupture a massive, pulsating red pimple on Toad's chest. The white pus burst out and Shawn eagerly ate it up.

"What the fuck!" Chuck's knuckles found Shawn's face

first, knocked him out of the way, but when the guy hit the ground, he was smiling, giggling. Then Toad's shirt was bunched up in Chuck's fists, and he lifted the little fucker right off his feet.

Toad had a strange look to him too, eyes soft and lazy, no sign of fear as Chuck tightened his grip and glared into the nerd's face. There was something tickling the back of his mind though, something that told him he didn't want to hurt Toad, that he needed him. That he should protect him instead, make sure nothing ever happened to him.

But he fought the alien thoughts away, cocked his head back, and thrust it forward. His forehead smashed into the middle of Toad's forehead, popping at least three zits there, splattering his flesh with red and white. The nerd hit the ground then, his dreamy fucking expression gone, pain taking over. The boy clutched his face, and Chuck mounted him, sat right on his stomach and was ready to pummel his head into a smear.

Hands and fingers and arms tried to fight him off, but not to stop him from hurting Kip. They wanted Chuck out of the way so they could get at the kid's skin. They called for the pus, begged to have that acne in their mouths.

Is everybody fucking insane all of a sudden?

Toad's eyes widened when he saw Chuck raise both fists in the air.

And then cold metal touched Chuck's temple, pressed hard.

"Get the fuck off him. Now."

Chuck didn't have to turn his head to know it was Zak. The other kids ignored the gun, and Zak pulled the barrel away from Chuck's head long enough to fire a round into the ceiling, then placed the now hot metal back to Chuck's temple.

Now the kids were all backing away, leaving Chuck alone on top of Toad.

"Get the fuck off, asshole."

Chuck held his hands up and moved away. He backed up, keeping his eyes on Zak until he collided with the wall of bodies behind him. The rest of the students shook, still called out for Kip, but didn't dare move toward him.

Jerrod and Cash still stood by the door, and Zak pointed his gun at them, jabbed the air with it.

"Move the fuck outta the way."

They did, joined the rest of the students on the other side of the house. In that small moment when the gun was pointed the other direction, some of the kids moved toward Toad again, licking their lips and caressing themselves. One of them was Jade, another Chelsea.

When Zak saw them approaching, he swung the gun back toward them, had to fire another bullet to get their full attention. The girls and the rest of the kids moved back.

Zak collected the Toad and ran off. Tires peeled out only seconds later.

The kids that didn't get a taste crumbled to the floor, pounding fists and kicking, scraping nails across their faces and crying out for Kip to come back. The ones who swallowed mouthfuls of pus still undulated on the floor, a few couples fucking and sucking and kissing and rubbing.

Chuck turned toward the crowd, found Jade and Chelsea pressed against the far corner, Jade crouched just in front of Chelsea, licking, tickling. Chelsea grinned and bucked, then her eyes popped open and she glared at Chuck, and he knew he should have been pissed to see his girls going at it like that, leaving him out completely.

But the tingling on his forehead wouldn't let him focus on anything else. It felt like a thousand electric maggots wiggling into his skin, and he blinked slow, smiled. Just a second ago, he was ready to pound Kip's face into pulp. But now…now he wanted the kid back. Never wanted him to leave again. Not ever.

Chuck wiped his hand across his forehead. Wet. Thick.

The inside of his fingers was painted red and white, smearing together into a pink sludge. He gave it a long sniff before running his tongue across the goop, letting it marinate his mouth and tongue and gums and throat.

Chelsea smiled, motioned for him to come to her with

her finger. Jade pulled her face away, now glistening, and she raised an eyebrow at him, let her tongue slide across her incisors.

As the pulsating high took over his body, Chuck dove right in.

CHAPTER SEVEN

"Where are we going?" Kip opened the passenger door, looked ready to jump from the car.

"Close the fucking door, man! Kip…come on."

Kip eyed the street as it sped by under the car, then finally slammed the door shut again, faced Zak and flailed his arms. "You have to take me back! Why are we leaving!"

Before Zak could answer, Kip growled and flung himself forward. His left shoulder slammed into Zak, made the car swerve, then Kip reached out and grabbed the steering wheel with both hands, tried to spin it back the other direction. Zak held on tight, slammed on the brakes, hit a curb and rolled the front driver's wheel over it.

He threw Kip back toward the passenger side, and when his cousin roared again, threw himself back toward the steering wheel, Zak threw a punch that landed right on the kid's nose. Blood blossomed, zits popped. Pink paste oozed over Kip's face, and he cupped his nose, leaned back in his chair, moaned.

"I'm sorry! I didn't want to, Kip…but you're not yourself. What's the fucking matter with you? What the hell was that back there?"

The zits on the back of Kip's neck thumped and pulsed, the open wounds on his face, where the other kids had sucked the pus out, oozed blood.

What did he say about his acne? That it was super human?

Zak knew for damn sure that pimples didn't gyrate like that, and he had never seen one hold so much pus and blood before and yet pop so easily. And when Kip's zits popped, they were like small explosions, the pasty insides splashing out like tiny water balloons filled to capacity with curdled milk.

Kip could only cry as he cupped his face, finally pulled it

away and stared at the blood filling his palms. "Y-you broke it. You fucking b-broke my nose."

"Well you fucking needed it! Now answer me...*what the fuck is going on!*"

"I don't know," Kip said through his sobs. "I have no idea, Zak. All I know is that they liked me. For once in my life, they actually liked me. They wanted me. Did you hear them calling my name? Did you see how much they *needed* me?"

Yes, Zak certainly did. And he stared at the pink goo on his knuckles and nearly licked them clean, but wiped his hand off on his jeans instead. "Kip, something weird's going on. Can't you see that?"

Kip breathed hard as he stared at Zak, his mouth propped open as he gasped, blood staining his teeth, tears and blood and pus glistening on his face. He looked like someone else, like a monster who had killed Kip and was now wearing his face.

But as Zak stared into Kip's face, the boy's expression softened. It was like whatever trance he was in, he just snapped right out of it.

"Zak...I'm scared."

"Me too. None of this feels real...can't be possible."

Kip crossed his arms, stared at the glove compartment, through it. "I'm a freak. That's what. I'm not normal. What was happening to them? Why were they acting like that?"

Zak wanted to tell Kip not to call himself a freak, but at the moment, Zak had to agree. "It was your acne. The pus. Something in the pus was making them crazy. Like a strong drug or something. And you too, Kip. You had this look on your face...shit, man, it fucking scared me. Still scares me."

"It's like I barely remember what happened. I mean...I remember Jade kissing me. I remember her freaking out and shoving me. Then everything is kind of a blur after that. I know they wanted me...I can remember them reaching out for me and calling my name. It was like a weird dream."

"It was bad. I thought they were gonna eat you alive, man. Like fucking zombies or something. And then that fucker

Chuck shows up with his buddies, all three of them smashed out of their minds. I had to use my gun…I'm sorry, cousin. It was either that or—"

"The bang. I remember the bang. Did you shoot someone?"

"Just the ceiling. Twice. Then I got us the fuck out of there."

Kip nodded. "Good. What do we do now? Ow…my nose hurts. My head too."

Zak pulled up to a red light, then leaned over and inspected Kip's nose. "Doesn't look broken, just busted up a little. I'm sorry."

"It's okay." He squinted, glared at the blood on his hands. "Am I some kind of monster or something? What if I'm an alien?"

"Shut up with all that shit, will you?"

"Well what then? I never knew my dad, and when I ask my mom about him, she just changes the subject. What if my dad wasn't human? A demon or something?"

"Slow down, Kip. You just called yourself a freak, a monster, an alien, and now a demon. How do you know this kind of thing hasn't happened before? Maybe we should be talking to a dermatologist or something."

But Kip just shook his head. "I've spent enough time with those people. If this was something normal, they would have said something by now. No…this is something else. Something big. And I'm terrified to know what it is."

"What if it's some kind of side effect from those pills you've been taking? That seems more plausible than fucking aliens and demons."

Kip didn't seem to like that possibility, like it wasn't dramatic enough. He just stared at the dashboard and frowned. "Maybe. I guess…"

Zak sighed, lit a cigarette.

"Me too. Please…"

Zak handed the lit cigarette to Kip, then lit another for himself. "Well we have to talk to *someone*. Maybe we should call the police…you know. Just in case people start trying to come to the house or something. Do the other kids know where you live?"

"In a town this small, everyone knows where everyone lives. Plus…there's only one Toad. Every now and then the house will get toilet papered or egged or spraypainted. Yeah…they know where I live."

"Well shit, man. Maybe we should stay at a motel. At least just for tonight. Maybe once they all come down off… off their high or whatever, they'll forget about it. Or at least come to their senses."

Kip just shrugged. "If that makes you feel safer, then that's fine with me."

"Aren't you scared? That was some fucked up shit, man."

Kip didn't answer. He smoked his cigarette and stared out the window.

Kip had lied. He remembered everything. There was no blur, no blackout.

He *had* felt like he was in a sort of trance, but he had still been in control. And he had never felt more amazing in his entire life. God, just thinking about Jade's soft body against his, the way her hard nipples poked him, the way her tongue swirled within his mouth. Every part of him wanted to go back to the party. He was a god there. The kids were his worshippers, and they needed him.

Kip didn't blame Zak for freaking out, though. He had to admit it was a little much to take in. At first, it didn't seem real, and he was sure he had passed out and slipped into some intense wet dream. But once he knew for sure it was really happening, it just felt right. Like it was what he was meant to do. As if all the teasing, all the ridicule and mental torture had been leading up to this moment, this occasion.

The craters on his face, neck, and chest that used to be bulging zits rippled, and he could still feel the sensation of the kids sucking the pus out, sliding their tongues over his flesh.

They called for me. They couldn't get enough of me. I'm not a toad anymore. I'm a fucking god. I'm their entire fucking universe now.

Kip finished his cigarette and flicked the butt out the window, then side-eyed Zak. He wondered if maybe his cousin was jealous of all the attention Kip was getting. Zak, the good looking new kid, the David Beckham look-alike. A guy who had never once had to worry about his appearance, never had to stress about girls because they always flocked to him. The guy who showed up at Bowie High and was fucking the hottest girl in school in less than a week.

That's what it is. He's jealous. He can't stand that they want me now...not him. Well I won't let him stop me.

Kip's flesh got to vibrating again, and he caught himself making himself angrier and angrier as he glared at the side of Zak's face. Kip unclenched his fists, relaxed his jaw. His skin stopped thrashing, slowed to a standstill.

No. No, not Zak. Zak's my only friend. My best friend. He wouldn't do that.

"You all right?" Zak used the butt of his first cigarette to light another. He offered another to Kip but Kip waved it off. "You look deep in thought."

"I am. Still trying to figure out why this is happening and what it all means."

"Well, whatever it is, I think you need to be careful. Whatever is inside of your acne...it's potent. Works faster than any drug I've ever seen, man. Those kids were jonesing for it. I've seen that look before. And there's something else too..."

"What?"

"I felt it too. Like I wanted to pop your pimples and suck the juice right out. I swear that's how I felt, for a little bit anyway. I was just as bad as the rest, but I sort of snapped out of it. Probably because I was so worried about you, cousin. Didn't want anything to happen to you."

"Really? But you didn't, right? How could you crave it if you didn't try it?"

"I don't know. It was something in the air, like your body was releasing some kind of chemical. Just being in that room almost made me crazy. And I'm no homo, but cousin, I wanted to lick your skin."

Kip sort of chuckled. "You don't…I mean. You don't still want to, do you? Because if you want to try it, I can—"

"No! Are you fucking kidding me right now?"

"Of course I am…I was, I was just fucking with you." He wasn't. He wanted Zak to try it, wanted his cousin to feel what the others felt.

"I hope so. You saw what it did to those other kids, Kip. Don't mess around. This is no fucking joke, okay? Promise me."

"Promise you what?"

"Promise me that you won't let them have any more. It's too dangerous…we don't know what we're dealing with here. Okay?"

Kip snorted, shook his head. He stared out the window but could see Zak's refection staring at the back of his head.

"It's not even a big deal. I don't understand why you're—"

"Fucking promise me, Kip. I'm not kidding around here. Don't do that shit anymore, no matter what, okay? *All right?*"

"Okay! *Okay!* Happy now? What, do you think I'm an idiot?"

"You don't remember. You didn't see what I saw. This is bad. This is so fucking bad."

They didn't say another word the rest of the drive. Zak pulled into the first hotel they saw, parked around back so his car couldn't be seen from the street. Kip offered to pay for his own room, but Zak insisted that they share a room.

He doesn't trust me.

And for good reason too. As soon as he got the chance, Kip had planned on running right back to the party, back to his people. But now that plan was ruined. Kip even thought about popping one of his zits into Zak's mouth once he had fallen asleep, turn him into one of his followers like the others, but ultimately decided against it. Zak was only trying to help, Kip knew.

As Kip lay on his bed, staring at the ceiling, he could feel the emptied pockets of flesh filling back up. The wounds tingled, felt electrified as the pus bubbled in and swelled the red skin back up to bulging. He wondered if his chemicals could be sensed from this distance, if the kids would be able to sniff him out. He hoped so.

He missed the feel of Jade's body. Her mouth. Her roaming hands. He missed all the groping fingers and mouths of the others too, boy or girl. Kip was no homo either, but even when the males had their mouths on him, drinking in his fluid, it felt so fucking good. Not in a sexual way really, but in some other way. Maybe like a mother feels when she's breast feeding her child. Kip didn't know for sure. He only knew that he wanted to feel it again. And again and again and again.

For the first time in his entire life, he couldn't wait for school in the morning.

CHAPTER EIGHT

Kip stood over Zak, nudging him in the ribs.

"What? W-what is it?"

"It's time for school. I want to stop by the house before we go in, change clothes, get my books."

Zak sat up, sanded his face with both palms as he yawned. "Shit, I completely forgot about that."

"Yeah, well…" Kip rocked from heel to toe. "We don't have much time. Let's get moving. I don't want to be late. For class."

Zak eyed him, brow lowered. "I think maybe we should stay home today, don't you?"

"Skip again? No. One day was bad enough. We're not skipping again, Zak. You promised me that—"

"I know, I know. But after last night…do you think it's smart to show up there? What if the other kids…you know…?"

"What? Suck my pus out? It's school, Zak. Nothing like that's going to happen, all right?" Kip flung the door open, letting in a tsunami of light.

Zak threw the sheet over his head and groaned. "Jesus. Okay, I'm up. Close the fucking door."

"Hurry up. I just know Mrs. Snodgrass is going to pop a quiz on us today. I want to cram before class."

Kip hoped there was a quiz that day. Anytime Mrs. Snodgrass surprised them with a pop quiz, that's when Gwendolyn usually spoke to him the most.

God, if she was only there last night. She could have seen the new me. She could have seen me be a real man.

She could have tasted me.

But she would know soon enough. Kip didn't know how he'd bring it up to her yet, but all he had to do was get her to

86

try some of his pus. Just a small sample, and she'd be hooked. Just like Jade. As much as Kip enjoyed Jade, as much as he ached to feel her again, he would toss her aside in a heartbeat if Gwendolyn showed any interest.

I can have anyone I want. But I only want her.

Zak lazily slid into his clothes, already had a lit cigarette dangling from his lips.

"Do you think any of them will remember last night? Everything that happened?" Kip said.

"I don't know. Maybe it's like Rohypnol or something. They might not remember shit, just all woke up naked on the floor in the middle of the night, confused and lost. I hope that's what happens."

They were walking down the cement steps toward the parking lot, and Kip stopped midway, spun so he was facing Zak.

"Why would you say that?"

"Why? Because that shit was insane. You telling me you want all of them trying to drink the pus right out of your skin like that?"

Kip squinted. "It's better than being called Toad all the time. Better than feeling like my only friend is my mom, that I'm so fucking disgusting that nobody even wants to hang out with me. I've never felt wanted before, like I belonged, until last night. Why is that such a bad thing?"

Zak flicked his cigarette. "Thought you said you don't remember."

"I remember enough to know it might not be such an awful thing. I'm just saying."

Zak checked them out of their room, and when he walked back outside, Kip was already sitting in the passenger seat. Zak slid in, started driving home.

"Kip…think about this, okay? Having every kid in school addicted to…you know. Addicted to your acne I guess… fuck, that sounds so crazy. It won't be good, man. You're just one guy. What happens when they suck it all up, when there's nothing left? What then?"

When they finally pulled up to the house, Kip sighed. He

almost showed Zak that all the pimples that had been emptied last night were already full again. They weren't ready to pop quite yet, but nearly there. Kip didn't think he'd ever run out, could supply the students with as much as they wanted.

But he didn't want to argue with Zak. His cousin was only worried about him, only wanted to protect him.

He's not jealous, Kip. No way. Not Zak. Zak's different than all the rest. The only one to ever stand up for you.

"You're right, Zak. My head's all screwed up, man. I remember enough about last night to know that it felt good. I'll admit that. Having them begging for me like that felt good. And of course...Jade."

"Oh yeah. And normally I would be congratulating you, cousin, but she wasn't herself. She was like a fucking junkie...they all were."

"I know that. But either way, it was my first time kissing a girl. First time touching one, really, except for in the hallways at school, and that's just by accident."

Zak smiled, reached over and squeezed Kip's shoulder. It felt good.

"God, she practically fucked you right in front of everyone. I couldn't believe what I was seeing."

"You? How do you think I felt? I'm still not convinced last night was real, you know?"

"Well, it was real. Let's just hope the kids don't remember."

"Yeah...yeah, let's hope so. I guess..."

They quickly got changed, Zak jumping into the shower. Kip didn't bother. He didn't want to wash the oil off, didn't want to cover up his scent with soap.

His people were waiting for him, he could feel them. They remembered. And they wanted him more than ever.

CHAPTER NINE

Zak couldn't concentrate. No matter how hard he tried. The images from last night swirled through his mind like rubble in a tornado, and the teacher's lecture might as well have been complete gibberish.

He looked at the students around him, studied their faces. As far as he could tell, everyone looked normal. Then again, there were only a select few who were at the party. The "popular crowd."

Shawn sat toward the rear of the class. Zak remembered seeing this kid sucking on Kip's neck, saw his lips stained red as he slurped up the white, creamy treat. But it looked like he was taking notes. The kid had bags under his eyes, kept yawning every few minutes, but nothing unusual for the day after a party.

"Zak?"

At the sound of his name, Zak flinched, elicited some giggles from the other students, especially the girls. The teacher stared at him, eyebrows high on his forehead, chalk pinched between finger and thumb, holding it out as if he wanted Zak to take it.

"What? I'm sorry…w-what?"

More laughter. The teacher pursed his lips, shook his head.

"Senior Skip Day. What a glorious tradition," the teacher said. "Now, if you can pull your head out from between your butt cheeks, will you kindly walk to the blackboard and solve this problem?"

Zak forced a smile, nodded. His head was so out of it today, he had nearly forgotten which class he was in. But the problem on the board, looking like a tower of random numbers and letters, let him know he was in his dreaded Algebra class.

"Solve for X, please."

"Yes, sir."

The girls looked him up and down as he trudged toward the front of the class, took the chalk from the teacher's hand with shaking fingers. He faced the blackboard, and felt himself sinking, melting like an ice cube in a frying pan. The problem was complete Greek to him, and no matter how hard he stared, no matter how hard he tried to remember how to do it, nothing came to him. And he just stood there, looking stupid and feeling stupider.

"Sometime during this period would be great," the teacher said.

"I…uh…I can't. I don't know how, sir."

The teacher shook his head, yanked the chalk from Zak's hand. Zak started to head back to his seat, but the man stopped him.

"Wait a minute, now. Maybe if you stand closer to the problem as I solve it, it may sink in better, hmm?" The man's hand worked rapidly, and he spat some equation that Zak was apparently supposed to remember, and just like that, he had an answer. Zak was as lost as ever.

"Just take your seat."

"Yes, sir."

Zak caught sight of Shawn, and the boy was still writing furiously, concentrating hard on the paper in front of him. His hand looked white from gripping the pen so hard, sweat beading and trickling over his face. His tongue kept darting from between his lips, sliding across the chapped skin, soaking in the moisture on his upper lip.

Zak took another long look at the students, and recognized one of the girls. She had been one of the three who greeted Zak and Kip just as they had arrived at the party. One of the bridge trolls. She sat in the furthest corner, and she also scribbled like mad on a sheet of paper. Her hair was in tangles, disheveled, and she bared her teeth as she worked her pencil back and forth across the paper. She wasn't taking any notes, but looked like she was drawing something, or rather etching it in.

The bell rang. Zak stood, started to head toward Shawn and the girl, but was grabbed by his elbow. He turned, expecting to see the teacher there shaking his head and smirking, maybe demanding that Zak try harder or something along those lines.

But instead, he looked into the face of a girl. He had never met this girl, though he had noticed her around here and there. Couldn't remember her name. Something about her was intoxicating though. Her face was devoid of any makeup, and she wore a simple loose-fitting shirt and jeans.

Zak couldn't help but smile, and he shot quick glances at Shawn and the girl as they exited the classroom, both looking jittery and sick.

"Hi," the girl said. "I'm Gwendolyn. You're Zak, right?"

Zak glared into the hallway, noticed a few of the other partiers passing by, each one looking on edge, ready to tear their hair from their scalps. Zak was suddenly filled with the urgent need to find Kip, make sure he was okay.

"Um...hello? Am I bothering you?"

"God...my head's all over the place today. Sorry. Yeah... I'm Zak. How'd you know that?"

She blushed, sort of tilted her head and puckered her lips. "Dude...you have to know. Every chick in this school is pretty much drooling over you. The mysterious new guy. *Ohhhhh.*" She waved her hands like she was telling a ghost story.

"Okay, okay. I might have noticed something like that."

"Yeah, I bet. Well...also your cousin Kip has mentioned you before. That kid thinks the world of you, you know that?"

"You know Kip? You must be that girl he mentioned."

"Oh yeah? And what did he say?"

Zak almost said it, but decided to hold his tongue. If this was the girl his cousin was so obsessed over, he didn't dare embarrass him. "Nothing really. Just said you talked to him. Not many people do, you know."

"Yeah...I know. He's a sweet kid. Smart as shit, too."

"I hear shit's pretty smart around here."

She punched him in the arm, hard enough to kind of hurt.

"Anyway, I feel bad for him. So I'll talk with him sometimes. Had to stand up for him when that fuckhead Chuck was giving him shit the other day. If I was a man, I'd ass rape that fucker."

Zak burst out laughing.

"What?"

"You've got an interesting choice in vocabulary, you know that? It's kind of refreshing to be honest."

She just shrugged. "Kip may have mentioned that his big, bad, and cool-as-hell cousin was coming to town, to stay with him and his mom. Got into some trouble back home?"

Zak's smile faded. "I guess you could say that, yeah."

"I didn't mean to pry like that. Look, the only reason I even bugged you at all was to let you know that I'm kind of smart as shit too. Especially in math. If you needed some help, or wanted me to tutor you or something…no charge of course…I'd be glad to. Unless Kip already is."

Her face suddenly glowed pink and she could barely look Zak in the eye.

"Yeah, that'd be nice. Kip's…busy these days. And since we're in the same class, it would probably do me good, right?"

"Yeah. Yeah, right."

"I'm warning you, Gwendolyn. When it comes to that algebra shit…I'm kind of a retard. I'm completely lost. It's hopeless, I'm telling you."

She hit him again, same spot. He couldn't hold back his hiss.

"It's not as hard as you think. And I'm a good teacher too. So…wanna meet up today? After school? We could meet at the library or…someplace else."

"How about the Grease Shack? I have to be honest…not really eager to stick around this place longer than I have to. I'll buy you a burger."

"Okay, yeah. You'll be a math genius in no time. Smarter than the stinkiest of shit."

Gwendolyn shot him another smile, brushed him with her left arm as she walked away.

Zak's heart was pounding. There was just something

about that girl, and he immediately couldn't wait to see her again.

"Zak!"

Chuck's voice. Fuck me. Here we go.

Zak turned, hands balled up at his sides. He bounced on his feet a little, ready to do what he had to.

But Chuck had no ill intent written on his face as he jogged down the hall toward Zak. His face was a mess, white crust fanned out from both corners of his mouth. Yellow muck sat in his eyes, and they sat deep in the dark circles of his sockets. Chuck actually smiled when he reached Zak, like they were old friends who hadn't seen each other in a while.

"Hey, man," Chuck said, out of breath.

"Chuck. You look like shit."

Chuck just laughed. "You s-seen Kip around? I've been looking all over for him and...I just really need to see him, man."

"Why do you need to see him?" Zak crossed his arms and squinted.

"I just..." Chuck stopped short, eyes moving to the ground and rolling around as he thought of some bogus excuse. "I want to apologize. You know...for how I've treated him. It wasn't right and I know that now."

"Really?"

Chuck nodded, smiled like a special ed student.

"What made you change your attitude? I had to put a gun to your fucking head just last night so you wouldn't kill the kid. Now this? Tell me what the fuck is going on, Chuck. No bullshit."

Chuck groaned, ran both palms over his face. He looked on the verge of crying. "If I tell you...if I tell you, will you bring me to him?"

Zak didn't answer, just stared hard.

"I need him. I fucking need him so bad."

"Because of what happened last night, right?" Zak looked over his shoulder, all around them to make sure nobody was listening. He leaned in closer to Chuck. "Because of the pus?"

Chuck's eyes widened along with his grin, and he nodded

93

so hard it looked like his neck would break. "Yes. Yes, the pus. Fuck, man…I need it. I'll die without it."

Chuck scratched at his cheeks, neck, and chest, baring his teeth.

"And Chelsea too. She's got it bad. She didn't come to school today…told me if I don't bring her back any more, she'd kill herself. I have to find Kip, Zak. Please help me."

Chuck had taken another step toward Zak, and their torsos pressed up against each other. Zak shoved him away, and Chuck's eyes softened. He dropped to his knees, grabbed the loose fabric of Zak's jeans over his shins.

"Please. *Please!*"

"Get the fuck off me," Zak said and kicked Chuck in the chest.

Chuck landed on his ass, cupped his face in his hands, and wept.

"What's going on here?" The math teacher. The man scowled at Zak, but when his eyes landed on Chuck, he smirked. He was about to walk away, as if the school's most popular jock deserved an ass kicking, but when Zak noticed the papers in the teacher's hand, he grabbed the man's arm.

"What's that?"

The teacher yanked his arm away, looked Zak up and down. "Not anything that concerns you. You need to be concentrating on your schoolwork."

"I just hired a tutor, literally a few minutes after class, sir. I'm trying."

The teacher looked ready to launch another verbal attack, but sighed, pursed his lips. He watched Chuck cry for another few seconds, then showed the papers to Zak. "Just a couple of papers I found on two of the students' desks. They look threatening to me, so I was going to show them to the principal. He's your cousin, right? Maybe you'd better warn him."

"Yeah…right."

The teacher walked off, taking the papers with him. Scratched into the college ruled notebook paper in black pen and gray lead was the word TOAD. Written over and over and over again, until every inch of the paper was covered, torn in places where they had pressed down too hard.

A hand gripped Zak's leg again.

"Zak, I'll do anything. I woke up this morning and all I could think about was Kip. That's all anyone could think about. Jade was the worst. She—"

"Where is Jade?"

Jade sucked on Kip's chest in the back seat of Zak's car. Kip ran his fingers through her hair and moaned as her teeth scraped across his skin and peeled back the oily membranes at the peak of each zit. She slurped up the cream like raw clams, rubbing her bare, wet pussy over his knee, fucking it. Her thumbnails popped the boils on his neck, and she pressed her nose to them, snorted, rocked harder and growled.

Kip was fully erect, his cock pressing up against her chest, her breasts rubbing against it in a constant up and down motion as she gorged herself on his discharge.

But he didn't want to take it out of his pants. If he did that, she might start playing with it, sucking it, and he didn't want that. Nothing could have possibly felt better than Jade feasting on his pus, breaking his skin to get to the treats inside. If she started on his dick, she would have to stop popping pimples, and he didn't even want her to stop. She had offered already, but he refused.

"Just keep…just keep doing what you're doing."

"Anything. Anything you say." Her eyes were almost completely white, as if she was engulfed in so much ecstasy, she couldn't unroll them from the back of her head. Her teeth chattered and her entire body spewed sweat, dripping down over Kip's torso only to be sucked up by Jade along with his oils and secretions.

Though her mouth stayed on his chest, her hand still coasted to the bulge in his jeans, massaged the head.

"No," he said. He moved her hand to his face, used her fingertips for her to pop a zit on his left nostril. The pus blew like water from a whale's blowhole, sprayed her in the face. And she gasped, licked it up like a kid licking cupcake frosting from their lips. Her hips rocked more violently, fucking his knee, drenching it in sex juice, and she tilted her head back and screamed, slammed her palms on the car's roof. A surge of warm fluid spilled over his knee, trickled down his thigh and soaked into his jeans.

She collapsed backward, banging the back of her head against the car window. Her hands were at her tits, rubbing her stomach, then down to her sex. Eyes still white, teeth still chattering. Something like a growl rattled from her mouth, and for a second, Kip worried she was having some kind of seizure, but then her pupils rolled to the front of her eyes and she smiled at him.

"I think...I think I fucking love you, Kip. My perfect little Toad."

At one time, that name infuriated Kip. Made him feel like a loser, like a freak. But now...now it just seemed to fit, had a new meaning.

Blood covered his chest and face, and he used Jade's shirt to sop it up. She didn't protest, just watched him and fingered herself, her tongue never staying still as it searched the nooks and crannies of her mouth for more pus.

Kip's body tingled from scalp to toenails, and it wasn't until he scooted back and into a seated position that he realized he had cum in his pants. Every time he pressed the shirt to his open zit wounds, he gasped as electric pulses of pleasure zapped him.

The car's clock told him he had about three minutes to make it to his next class.

"I've got to go."

"G-go? Where? Why?" She flung herself forward like a jaguar attacking its prey, latched her claws into his thighs and held him there. "Kip, no. Don't leave me. I don't ever want you to leave me."

"Relax. I'll see you after school, okay? My mom's out of town...you can come by."

She looked on the verge of tears, and then her expression changed into something else. Something violent. "I need you. Do you understand? *I fucking need you!*"

Kip leaned forward, popped another pimple on his temple, offered the pus on the tip of his finger.

Jade gasped, sucked his finger into her mouth down to the knuckle. She moved her head back and forth, swirled her tongue over it. When she screamed with orgasm, Kip slid out of the car, hurried across the parking lot toward campus.

But there were others waiting for him. Others who had seen him in the car with Jade. They had stayed hidden, but as soon as Kip was out of the car, they started to close in like a swarm of flies on a rotting dog carcass.

"Toad…Toad come here. Please. I just…I just wanna talk to you."

"I've been looking for you all day, man. I can't stop *thinking* about you."

"Please, Kip. Please give me another taste."

"I have to go to class," Kip said, throwing his hands up. "I'll see you guys later, okay?" Kip picked up his pace, weaving his way through the kids. There was a scream from behind him, and he stopped, turned.

Jade was out of the car now, still wearing nothing, and had another girl by the hair, slamming her face into the parking lot cement again and again. Blood painted the girl's face, but her eyes were on Kip, her hand reaching out to him.

"He's mine," Jade said. *"He's all mine! My Toad, my Toad, my Toad!"*

Holy shit. They really need me. They need me bad.

Kip could already hear Zak's voice in his head, telling him how bad all of this was, how they needed to get away from it. And deep down, Kip knew that would be the right thing to do. The smart thing.

But he was done doing the right thing. He couldn't deprive his followers, his people. They needed him, wanted him, and he needed them just as bad.

"Kip!"

Kip thought he recognized the voice, and he turned to find Chuck sprinting toward him. At one time, seeing Chuck coming at him full speed would have filled him with dread, but he only smiled as Chuck pumped his arms and legs. When

Chuck made it to him, he dropped to his knees, grabbed Kip's hand, pressed his forehead against the knuckles.

"Kip...please. I need more. I have to have it, okay? Kip—"

"Call me Toad."

And he led his flock away from the school.

CHAPTER TEN

School was out.

Thank god.

Zak waited by his car for Kip, but it had already been fifteen minutes since the bell rang, and the kid wasn't showing. Zak had just finished the last cigarette, so he opened the car to fish out the fresh pack, but nearly gagged at the scent that floated out and punched him in the face.

Smelled like pussy and bad meat.

That's when he noticed the specks of red on his window. And the discarded clothing on the floor, the shirt—which was obviously female—stained with dark blood.

Kip. And probably Jade.

Zak breathed to calm his nerves, tried to tell himself that he was jumping to conclusions, that Kip would come walking up any second. He gave it another five minute before he couldn't take it anymore, before he jumped in the car, all the windows down, and sped toward home.

If Zak found what he thought he would, he wasn't really sure what he would do. Whatever was in Kip's pus, it was strong shit. No telling how it was affecting the kids, what it would make them do. After only a taste last night, they had that meth head look, like if they didn't get another hit they would die. Or kill. It was that last part that worried Zak.

I'll point my gun at them again if I have to. Whatever it takes to get them away from Kip.

He had a vision of walking in to the home, finding blood splashed and smeared all over the walls. The kids would have Kip on the ground, surrounding him live feasting buzzards, his torso ripped open, the kids chewing his flesh, sucking out his juices.

If any of them hurt Kip, I'll fucking kill them.

Zak tried to understand where Kip was coming from. Living an entire life shunned by everyone, laughed at, harassed. Girls weren't just unattracted to him, they were disgusted by him, and they did nothing to hide the fact either. And then all of a sudden he's the most desired boy in school. The most popular. Everyone wants him now.

Zak couldn't blame the kid. If the circumstances were different, he'd even be happy for him. But this? Zak wondered if there was something to what Kip was saying. What if he really was some kind of…monster or something? There really wasn't any other explanation. Kids don't just spew drugs from their skin like that. No matter how dangerous some experimental medication is…the side effects can't be this.

Zak tried to clear his mind as he made the final turn toward the house, preparing himself for what he might find.

He tried to ignore the tingling sensation in his chest as he continued to breathe in the odor in his car. Tried to pretend that he didn't want a taste of the Toad just like everyone else.

Chuck didn't have time to go back and get Chelsea. He hadn't even thought of her until after he got his taste, and by then he didn't give a shit. She could fend for herself. It was her fault for staying home and not getting her own taste of the Toad. Chuck lay on his back in Kip's attic while the other kids swarmed around Kip, mouths pressed against him. Feeding, slurping, moaning. Like baby pigs fighting for their mother's teats.

Chuck couldn't help but giggle as the other kids fought for the fat zits, craving the pus, dying for another helping of warm cream.

But Chuck got himself a mouthful of blood this last time. There were too many others, and Chuck started to toss them away, muscle his way in, but Toad gave him a look, shook his head.

"Everyone gets their share," Toad had said.

And Chuck didn't want to upset him. There was an open spot on Toad's right side, just under his armpit. Chuck had dove for it, licked the trickling blood away just to wipe the spot clean so he could search for more of the pimples. But in that particular spot, there was none. The skin was dry, flaky, but no acne. No flesh grapes.

Then it was like his mouth was on fire. Like he'd taken a spoonful of ghost chili salsa. But only at first. He panicked, flopped on the ground as he scraped his nails across his tongue. But the pain blossomed into waves of pleasure, and as each wave hit him, crashed over his body like liquid lightning, he couldn't stop himself from giggling.

"Blood..." he managed to say before more giggles took over. "B-blood is good...his blood is good too..."

Then the ceiling started to move, like the surface of a pond after a rock had been thrown in. The rotating fan looked like a spinning octopus, and Chuck forced himself to his feet, climbed up onto Kip's bed, and reached for it.

"Okay...okay that's enough."

Chuck thought he heard Toad say that, but couldn't be sure. There was a whispery sensation in his ear, like a thousand ghosts telling him secrets at the same time. All Chuck could do in response was chuckle, bounce on the bed and reach for those tentacles.

He lost his footing, slammed the side of his face on the floor. A tooth rattled loose, slid across the floor on a slip-n-slide of blood. A crack splintered the enamel...no not a crack. A mouth. Then two more cracks—eyes. The tiny eyes were as bright as Maglites, and the mouth just kept saying the same phrase again and again.

"The Toad is yours. The Toad is yours."

"Mine," Chuck said as he peeled his face off the ground and rose to his feet. "The Toad is *mine!*"

The room swam. The air felt as thick as Jell-O. Chuck had to take each breath slow and easy, made more difficult by his constant giggles.

"Enough, you guys. Okay...please. It's starting to hurt... *please!*"

Toad? Is that Toad...in trouble?

Chuck looked down at himself. *When did I take my clothes off?*

101

But that didn't matter. Toad needed him. The other kids refused to stop feeding, and now Toad was screaming, throwing his arms and legs around like one of those inflatable wavy guys outside of the car dealership.

Chuck was going to help him. He wanted to help him.

"The Toad is mine…"

Once he got enough of the other kids out of the way, using his knuckles and elbows and head and teeth, he caught sight of Toad's bare chest. Deep craters where zits used to be, now only scooped out potholes of flesh and blood. And there was so much blood. It bubbled out, ran down Toad's body.

And Chuck pressed his tongue to Toad's skin and licked. Lapped up as much as he could. The others were already pawing at him from behind, clawing and scraping, doing everything they could to get their share.

Toad's body started to shake then. His eyes went white.

Chuck didn't think that was good, but he couldn't do anything but laugh. Some of the other kids sat on the ground and laughed too, and Chuck wondered if they had been drinking Toad's blood like he had been. A boy and a girl fucked on Toad's bed now, looked to Chuck like conjoined twins connected at the groin. When the boy reached up and squeezed the girls breasts, it looked like his hands plunged into her chest, his fingers starting to poke out through her back.

"Stop! What the fuck!"

Chuck turned to find Zak standing by the stairs, eyes wide, mouth hanging open.

"Zak!" Chuck said and cackled. "The Toad is mine!"

They love me. I am their entire universe.

The students could hardly wait to get their fix, and once Toad got them into his house, up into his room—his treehouse—he took a seat in his computer chair, pulled his shirt off, and held out both arms as if to hug them all at once.

"Go ahead," he said. "Take all you need."

Jade, of course, was head of the line. She straddled him first, swirled her tongue in his mouth and dry-humped him, moaning into his throat. Then she dismounted, circled around to his rear. She ran her nails down his back, slicing the zits open, then pressed her face there, simultaneously slurping and snorting. Kip wanted to watch her, but could only hear the wet, sloppy sounds of her smorgasbord.

The others attacked him then, punching and biting and kicking at each other to get the good spots. Kip tried to keep count of who got what, but after a couple of minutes, he couldn't differentiate one person from the other. He saw Jezebel and Sasha, Cash and Jerrod, other cheerleaders and jocks and cool kids. All from the party. All known as the popular crowd. The same kids who have been making Kip's life awful since the day he hit puberty and sprouted his acne. The same kids who would call him names and laugh at him and throw things at him. The same girls who would only look in his direction to wrinkle their nose or laugh or make jokes with their friends. They were all over him now, and he loved every second of it.

And then of course, there was Chuck.

Nothing filled Kip with more joy than seeing Chuck gorging himself on pus and blood. Crying for more. Begging for it. Kip contemplated refusing Chuck, shunning him. But he couldn't do that. Chuck was his now, and though the kid was Kip's worst enemy for years and years, it was different. He felt close to Chuck, to all of them. Like they were his children.

That's right. I'm the popular one now. You'll all die without me.

Kip closed his eyes and tilted his head back, enjoyed the infinite abyss of pleasure that he was now engulfed in. Every set of lips, every pinch of thumbnails or teeth, each one was like its own orgasm, and Kip shuddered as they all fed.

He didn't know how long they had been at it…but then something happened. Something changed.

The pleasure sprouted needles.

Suddenly, every time one of them sucked, bit, squeezed, his flesh reacted with pain. Hot, agonizing pain that started at the point of impact and buried deep into his meat, digging and digging deeper until it found his marrow.

"Okay…okay, that's enough."

103

But they wouldn't stop. He heard Chuck cackling like a mad man, bouncing on Kip's bed, his face and hands painted with blood. Others fucked or fought, but most were still attached to Kip's skin like ticks, never satisfied, never full.

Oh god...they're killing me. It hurts...it fucking hurts!

"More, baby. I want more...please."

That was Jade's voice, coming from behind him. He tried to turn his head to get a look at her, but couldn't manage it with all the bodies piled on top and around him.

"The Toad is mine!" Chuck screamed through a mouthful of laughter. He lay face-first on the floor, a splatter of blood painting the floor just beside his face like a crimson comic book text balloon.

Jade scraped her teeth across the back of Kip's neck, but the pimples there had already been used up, and she got a mouthful of blood, but seemed just as happy to have it.

My blood works too? Am I just some kind of drug factory or something?

Then Chuck rushed forward, slamming his giant fists into the heads and faces of the others, boy or girl. He grabbed one girl by the hair as he smashed a boy's nose sideways with his elbow. But the pain didn't seem to bother them. It was being pulled away from Kip that drove them crazy, and as soon as they unlatched, they would scream, growl, fight to get their place back.

Chuck slapped his tongue to Kip's chest, swirled it around and drank up the blood that poured down.

Jade had her mouth suctioned to the back of Kip's neck now, groaning as she drank and drank, making loud gulping sounds.

And then Kip was somewhere else. He could still feel the pain, could still feel the mouths and hands all over him. But he couldn't see the others anymore. Couldn't even see his own body. Everything was blackness, abyssal nothingness.

It felt like he was rolling in a bed of broken glass and soaked in sulfuric acid. He tried to scream but could only gurgle and cough and everything tasted like blood and bile and shit and all he wanted to do was be left alone and make everyone get off of him but they wouldn't because they needed him so bad and he wanted them to need him, wanted to give them all he could but it just hurt too bad like he didn't have anything left to give, as if they had drained his flesh dry.

The air felt like lava, splashing across his face and body and burning him away layer by layer.

No more...no more.

And then something brought him back to the here and now. Something familiar. Something that he knew would save him and make all the pain go away.

"Stop! What the fuck!"

Zak?

When Kip woke up, he was on his back. He was sure it was Zak's face he would see, Zak telling him that he would be okay, that he wouldn't let anyone hurt him anymore.

But it was Jade's face that materialized before his eyes. She wore a mask of blood, and it looked like she was trying to speak, but only wet sounds were coming out of her mouth as she giggled and clenched her teeth, eyes wide and insane.

Her tongue ran across her lips, and then she began to lower her face, long ribbons of crimson drool hanging from her mouth.

"No...no don't..." His voice was barely a whisper now, each word popping from his mouth like weak, thin-skinned bubbles.

Just before her lips touched his face, a foot came flying out of nowhere, collided with the side of Jade's head and made her disappear from Kip's view.

Kip managed to sit up. He was completely naked, covered in blood and open wounds. Bite marks covered his torso, but it was the scooped-out holes that bled the worst. The places where zits once were, sucked completely empty of their filling. His skin pulsated, and though the pain was intense, there was something else he could feel. Anger. Poisonous anger crackling across his flesh. It took over his every thought, brought him to his feet.

Zak was on the ground now, covering himself as the others stomped on him, punched him. Chuck screamed with

105

laughter as he rained down blows again and again, his entire body speckled or awash with blood.

"Enough," Kip said.

A pair of hands took him from behind, and Kip seized them, flung Jade around so she faced him. Her eyes were alive with hunger, need, and she squealed as she tried to get back to him. Kip reached out, grabbed her by the throat, pulled her toward him so they were eye to eye. She fought at first, but then went slack, looked like a child who just realized she was in trouble.

"I said...enough."

She nodded, lip quivering. When Kip let her go, she dropped, crawled away and whimpered like a kicked puppy.

A puddle of blood began to form at Kip's feet as more and more of it dripped from his body. His chest heaved as he breathed in and out, now almost enjoying the pain, using it to find strength to face the kids. His people...his addicts.

"I said that's enough!"

As he screamed, blood squirt from various wounds on his body, painted the walls, the floor, the ceiling.

All movement stopped. All eyes were on Kip.

"You've had enough. Leave."

Zak crawled away from them, jumped to his feet. He grimaced, but was still in one piece. He spat a wad of blood onto the floor, his eyes jumping from the group of stunned kids to Kip.

They all just stared, almost all of them now devoid of any clothing. Their skin was covered in Kip's fluids, and when he took a step toward them, they collectively flinched.

"I said leave!"

Jade was on her feet first, sprinting out of the room and charging down the stairs. The rest followed, thundering out of the house, leaving bloody footprints in their wake.

Kip strolled to his window, watched as the blood-drenched congregation ran down his street in all directions, tits and balls flapping.

"Kip," Zak said from behind him. "You motherfucker. You fucking—"

As soon as the kids were gone from Kip's view, the anger seemed to subside some, bringing his pain right back to the forefront. A strangled whimper burst from his lips as his knees turned to jelly beneath him, and he crumbled to the floor. The open wounds on his torso wept endless blood as this skin throbbed, constant throbbing.

"Kip?"

Kip could barely breathe as he rocked himself in a pool of his blood, praying for the pain to ease up, just a smidgeon, anything.

Then Zak was beside him, lifted him to his feet, draped Kip's arm over his shoulder and walked him down the attic steps, into the bathroom. Then Kip was in the tub, the back of his head resting on the hard porcelain, his blood swirling down the drain. Kip didn't know how much longer he could bleed like this before he bled completely out. Before the nothingness came back and ate him whole.

"Hold on, Kip. Just hold on."

Water hit him then, and though it was ice cold, it felt like fiery needles burrowing into him. He screamed and his mouth filled with water.

"I'm calling an ambulance."

Kip wanted to turn the water off, but he couldn't make himself move. Then the water became warmer, soothing. He breathed a sigh of relief, and in that same instant, the pain began to slowly fade away, replaced again by the euphoric vibrations. As the water pelted against him, he had to grab the edge of the tub as a powerful orgasm began in his stomach, spreading to his groin and legs.

Pearly seed spurted from his penis, which he just now realized was hard, and it mixed with the blood and swirled down the drain. Kip laughed. He ran his fingertips across the crater-ridden flesh of his chest and face, shuddering at the sensation, and he laughed and laughed.

"Yes! My cousin…something's wrong with him. I'm not sure! Just please…shit I don't even know. Hold on." Zak lowered the phone. "Kip…your address. What's your address!"

Kip spun his attention to his cousin who had his cell phone pressed against his ear, his eyes perfect circles, brow beginning to furrow as he studied Kip's face.

"No," Kip said through his laughter. "No ambulance. I feel great."

"What? Are you fucking…I'm trying, ma'am. I'm trying…" Zak dropped the phone at his side, stepped closer to Kip. "Kip, please. You need help. You need to be checked out, seriously. Look how much blood you lost already."

Kip only smiled and shook his head. "I promise, Zak. I've never felt better than I do right now. My body…it's regenerating. I can feel it. I'm better than ever, Zak. Hang up the phone."

"No. I won't. You're getting some help—"

"Hang up the fucking phone!"

Kip was on his feet before he knew it, and just that quickly, the anger was back, pumping through his bloodstream, making him want to cause pain, making him want to kill.

But not Zak. Never Zak. Right?

Zak backed away, the woman's voice barely audible through the phone as she shouted, asking, begging for the address. It looked at first like Zak had been hurt by Kip's outburst, but that look quickly twisted into a countenance of terror as he stared at Kip's chest, then finally rose a shaking finger, dropped the phone.

Kip already knew before he looked. He could feel it, could taste it with every breath he took.

"Y-your skin. What the fuck…" Zak stared at Kip the way people had been staring at him his whole adolescent life. Face full of disgust, revulsion.

Kip ran his hand over the new bumps there, each one nearly full again. The blood had slowed, nearly stopped completely now.

Kip stepped out of the tub, the water still hissing behind him as it sprayed from the showerhead. Zak took an equal step away from him.

"Zak…don't look at me like that. It's me…it's still me. It's Kip. Your cousin, remember?" Kip spun so he was facing the mirror, watched as the craters inflated like red bubbles over his face and chest, the skin thin and glistening as it pulsated. He could feel the flesh of his neck, back, and ass thrashing as well, could feel each new pimple filling back up with pus.

"Kip...what's going on? This...this can't be... We have to get you some help, man."

Kip wanted to laugh again, but he held it in. His cousin was scared, looked ready to run away screaming at any second. So Kip hid his glee, put on a scowl, leaned his forehead against the bathroom wall.

"Help me, Zak. I don't know what's wrong with me."

Zak glanced at the phone, was tempted to scoop it up and ask for help regardless of what Kip had said. He didn't know if the police would be able to trace a cell phone call to that address, but he hoped they could.

"Help me, Zak. I don't know what's wrong with me."

Kip sounded like himself again. A moment ago, he sounded like someone completely different, the same person that had roared at all the students in the attic, scared them so bad that they scattered like alley cats.

He sounded like a monster. A demon. His voice had been deeper, gruff, full of rage and venom.

But now, his dorky, frail cousin seemed to be back. Resting his head against the wall and weeping softly. As he did this, the flesh of his back boiled and bubbled, zits growing and bulging right before Zak's eyes.

"Kip," Zak said as he took a tentative step forward, placed a soft hand on Kip's shoulder. "We have to take you to someone, get you looked at. Something's fucked up here, man. Maybe a doctor can figure out what's going on. Maybe we should call your mom and—"

"No!" It was still Kip's voice, but with a hint of demon.

"Kip..."

"Please, Zak. She's worked so hard for this. We shouldn't bother her, okay? We can figure this out, me and you. And if it gets worse...okay. We'll see a doctor. But right now...I mean it. I feel great."

You feel great? Are you fucking serious! You almost bled to death! You look like a nightmare!

"I just don't see how it could possibly get any worse. I thought you were gonna die, man. I really did. Ah, fuck...my ribs. Chuck got me good." Zak grimaced as he massaged his side, then slid his tongue over the drying blood on his lower lip. Through all the excitement, all the worry for Kip's life, he had been numb to his own injuries. But they were reminding him of their existence now.

"Whatever's inside of me, they're crazy for it."

"Yeah, we've fucking figured that already. What did you think would be different this time, Kip? Don't try and tell me you didn't expect that shit."

"Not like this. It...it feels good. When they...you know, when they suck it out of me. It feels *good*. But then it started to hurt...I thought they were killing me."

"They almost did kill you."

"It's like I can't help it. It feels so good, I lose track of what's going on...lose track of my own existence. When they're feeding off me, I feel like a god, Zak. I can't explain it any better than that."

Kip sort of smiled when he said this, eyes blank and staring through the wall. He seemed to snap out of it, blinked rapidly before turning back to Zak.

"But I'm scared. I don't know what to do."

"Fucking get help. Maybe a doctor can't help, maybe a doctor will be just as confused as we are. But we won't know until we get you checked out." Zak wanted to grab Kip by the shoulders and shake him.

"I don't want to see a doctor."

"You can't be fucking serious. You like this shit, don't you? You don't want to see a doctor because you're scared they'll make it all go away, right? You're scared you'll just be the same old Kip, scared you'll be the Toad again."

"I am the Toad! I'll always be the fucking Toad!"

Zak backed up. Kip's skin frenzied now like boiling water.

"I'm scared of what the doctor will say to me, Zak. What

if I was right, huh? What if I'm not human or something."

"That's ridiculous."

"Is it? Why? Is it any more ridiculous than my acne spitting out addictive pus? Or my blood acting like some kind of fucking hallucinogen?"

Zak had no answer. *Hallucinogen?*

"And what if the doctors can't figure out? What then? They'll call in specialists, other doctors, and I'll turn into one big fucking science experiment. Well fuck that. I'm done with people treating me like I'm less than human. Because I'm not. I'm way more."

Kip stepped out of the bathroom into the hallway, his skin beginning to calm to a slow, rhythmic pulse. The blood was caked there, drying and flaking off as he moved.

"But, Zak, what happened today…that won't ever happen again. Okay? I promise."

Zak had so much that he wanted to say, but couldn't make his mouth move. He just nodded and watched as Kip walked back down the hall toward the attic where he ascended the stairs. Kip didn't pull the stairs back up behind him, and Zak wondered if Kip wanted him to follow, but there was no way in hell he was going back up there. The room had blood all over the place, discarded clothing, cum and sweat.

Zak had to concentrate to calm his breathing. There were stains on the bathroom wall spotted with Kip's blood. The spot where his forehead had been resting.

Zak stepped forward, sniffed the blood, eyelids fluttering and chest tingling.

I gotta get the fuck outta here.

He was in his car and heading down the street. No destination in mind, just needed to get the hell away from Kip and that house before he became just like everyone else. He wanted a drink, wanted some pills, wanted a big fat line of coke. But most of all…he wanted Kip. He wanted to taste what everyone else was tasting, experience the high that was driving them all crazy.

No. I can't…I can't ever.

He lit a cigarette with shaking fingers and just drove.

CHAPTER ELEVEN

"Chelsea, open this door!" *Pound pound pound.* "What's the matter with you?"

"Just leave me alone, Dad! P-please…"

Chelsea stared in the mirror, the flesh on both cheeks torn open by her own fingernails. Similar scratches and gouges decorated her arms and thighs, and even though the pain was awful, she dug her nails in and scratched, scraping away thin strips of meat from her face.

The scratches hurt, but it was nothing compared to the pain within. The pain that begged her for more of the Toad, for more of his pus.

Where the fuck is Chuck!

She didn't know how long ago he had left for school to find Kip and bring back more for them to share. He said he would be right back…but that son of a bitch never showed. He lied, *he lied!*

Chelsea screamed, smashed her fist into the mirror and cracked it, ignored the blood now dripping from her knuckles.

"Chelsea! That's enough, goddamit. If you don't open this door in the next five seconds, I'll bust it down myself! *Chelsea!*"

"Fuck you, Dad. Fuck you! *You don't understand! You'll never understand!*"

"Chelsea!" Her mother's voice. "What has gotten into you?"

Tears flowed from her eyes and thinned out the blood oozing from her wounds. She paced back and forth, her footsteps heavy and pounding. Her arms flailed as she knocked over her lamp, her books, her toys, her picture frames.

Chuck's smiling face stared up at her from the cracked frame just at her feet. A violent burst of sobbing took her then as she fell onto her ass, cradled the photo.

"Where are you, Chuck? You said you'd come back but you lied to me and I hate you but I love you so bad. Oh God... please, Chuck. Please."

Tap.

It came from the window.

Tap.

Chelsea gasped, jumped to her feet. Her sweatshorts were soaked with blood, and the carpet was spotted with it here and there.

"That's it, Chelsea. You hear me?" Her dad rattled the handle a few more times before the pounding started. She could hear her mother out there whimpering, trying to calm her father down. A weak fucking cunt, always was.

Chelsea figured he was going to try and break it down, but knew he wouldn't be able to do it. Not strong enough, too skinny, not like her Chuck, her sweet and beautiful Chuck who had come to her rescue at last. And there was no key to unlock her door either because he had swiped it and had it sitting on her dresser.

But none of that mattered anymore.

"Chuck? Is that you?" She flew to her window, threw it open, peered out. It was still day time, but it wouldn't be for much longer. The air was cool, felt good on her wounds, and when she saw Chuck's face smiling up at her, she nearly dove right out of the window to greet him.

He just stared up at her and giggled. His eyes looked bright against the dark red of his face.

Is that blood?

Chelsea quickly wondered if he'd been hurt, but didn't worry about it long. She needed to know if he had brought anything for her. Needed to know if he kept his promise to her. Because if he didn't...she would fucking kill him. She would tear his fucking nuts off.

And he just kept laughing.

"Will you hurry the fuck up? I'm dying in here. Please, Chuck!"

"His blood," Chuck said as he climbed the wooden lattice

wrapped in ivy toward her window. "His blood too. It works too. And it feeeeeeels *awesome!*"

When he gripped the windowsill, Chelsea grabbed hold of his forearms, ran her blood-caked nails across his flesh, trying to pull him in. He stumbled into the room, landed on top of her. He stank, the smell reminding Chelsea of roadkill and spoiled beef and…and Toad. That's what it reminded her of. The Toad.

"His blood too."

Chelsea didn't waste any time, ran her tongue across Chuck's face, his chest, his stomach, his cock and balls. Kip's blood was all over him. It burned, but it burned good. Tasted like fire and orgasm and relief.

"What about the zits? The pus? Did you b…b…"

She wanted to ask about the pus because it's all she'd been able to think about for what felt like forever and she wanted Chuck to stop fucking around and give it to her already but she couldn't get the words out as the blood too effect. Chuck's smiling face looked like it split in half, and a rainbow of colorful light spilled out like liquid crayons.

"The Toad is mine," Chuck said.

She's trying to take it from me. But…but it's mine.

After Chuck had left Toad's house, he was compelled to head to Chelsea's. Now that he was there, in her room, Chelsea underneath him and licking him clean, he couldn't remember why he came. He remembered why he left Toad's room, or rather ran from it. When Toad had shouted, blood squirting from his body in countless different places, Chuck had felt it in his guts, in his chest and head. It wasn't pain, but pure fear. When he heard Toad's voice, he just knew to run away, just knew to disobey him was to die. Or worse…be denied any more of him.

And now that he was in Chelsea's room, someone pounding on her bedroom door and shouting, he realized she was licking Toad's blood off him. Cleaning him. She cackled now, but wouldn't stop scraping her tongue over his skin, and when he saw his flesh tone instead of the red and maroon of Toad's blood, he slapped his palm into her face and tried to push her away but she fought back and outstretched her tongue, wiggled it in circles between his fingers to try and get another taste.

Toad's blood still swirled through his system, but it didn't feel the same. He needed more. And it wasn't until Chelsea started tongue-bathing him that he realized he was covered in it.

"No," he said and shoved her face harder, but she only pushed back harder in response. *"The Toad is mine, you stupid fucking bitch!"*

The pounding at the door got louder, so did the shouting. A man. Chuck didn't have time to worry about who it was or why they wanted in. He thought he heard a woman's voice too, but couldn't be sure.

It's more people trying to take the Toad away from me. But they can't have him because he's mine. He's all fucking mine!

Chelsea squirmed and snickered. Blood oozed out of deep scratches across her cheeks. She licked her lips, eyes wide and dilated. "Where is he, Chuck?" she said through her chortles. "Where is Toad? I *need* him."

Chuck still had his hand in her face when she started trying to lick him again, and he pulled the hand away only to replace it with his fist. Knuckles slammed against the bridge of her nose, cracking it, spraying blood over her lips and teeth and she just licked it up, seemed oblivious to her own pain, never stopped laughing.

So he hit her again. This one rocked her head back, and she stopped struggling for a few seconds, just writhed beneath him, her ruined face rocking from side to side. But she still giggled, still asked for another taste.

"You can't fucking have him!"

More pounding and pounding and screaming from the other side of the door.

Chuck reached out, grabbed something hard and flat just a few feet above Chelsea's head. He lifted it with both hands, brought it down as hard as he could to make this stupid

115

fucking cunt stop laughing already. So sick of hearing her laugh!

The sound was wet and crunchy when the metal hit her face, and he brought it over his head again, jammed it back down. Then again and again until she finally stopped moving, finally stopped *fucking laughing.*

Chuck stared at the object in his hand. A picture frame. His face smiling out. His school picture, his football picture. Now splattered with Chelsea's blood, the glass shattered. He remembered giving her that photo, and for a quick second, he remembered loving this girl, somewhere in the past he loved her.

The frame had split her mouth at the corners, busted out a lot of her teeth which floated and swam in the gurgling blood filling her mouth and spilling over the sides. Her lips looked like cooked ham and her tongue swirled in slow circles. Her eyes kept trying to roll to the back of her head, but then they locked on Chuck, quivered for a moment.

Gurgle...choke, choke...gurgle...

"Stop fucking laughing!"

He slammed the frame down one more time, lodging it in her mouth, pressing down with all his weight until he felt something break and crunch under him. Her body jumped once, legs rattled, then she stopped moving. The frame stayed upright when Chuck let go of it, then he stood, slammed his fists into his forehead as the yelling got louder and louder and the door rattled in its frame.

"Chelsea answer me! What's going on! Who's in there!"

Chuck roared, stomped toward the door, unlocked it.

When it flew open and Chuck saw the man standing there, a short, scared-looking woman clinging to his side, Chuck growled, launched himself forward.

The man yelped when they collided, and Chuck pushed, took the man off his feet. And then the man was gone, falling and falling, the back of his head slamming against a rail on his way down to the first floor.

Crack!

Blood pooled around his head and spread across the floor

quickly. The woman screamed, tried to run but Chuck caught her by the hair at the back of her head, dragged her across the floor only to pick her up and send her down to the first floor with her husband. The woman's landed on her feet, but her body folded in on itself on impact, and she lay on her side, just beside the man, screaming and screaming. The screams were sloppy and gruff, and Chuck almost ran down to make her shut up, but he went back into Chelsea's room instead, was just about to climb back out her window and go running back to Toad. He would beg Toad for more, get on his knees and just beg.

"Mommy?"

The voice came from the hallway, and then there was crying. Crying and screaming.

"Mommy! Daddy!"

"The Toad is mine!" Chuck ran his fingernails across his eyes as he sprinted back into the hallway.

Jade wept on the bedroom floor. She didn't understand why her Toad had been so mad at her. All she wanted to do was love him, love him forever and ever. She wanted to be with him, to go back to him, to feel him inside of her.

Not his cock…not like other boys. His soul, his essence. His fluids.

She got back to her feet and stared at the red mess on the bed. Daddy had tried to yell at her, tried to tell her that she was a whore, a good for nothing slut who was only good at one thing and that he would show her what she was good at just like he always did.

But Daddy can't have her anymore. She doesn't belong to him now. She belongs to Toad.

She tried to find her father's face in the pile of meat lying on the mattress, wanted to look him in the eye one last time, but she couldn't find it.

It doesn't matter. The only thing that matters is getting back to my love.

Blood painted her entire body, but she couldn't tell what was Toad's and what was her father's anymore. She licked

117

her arm, swallowed, but it wasn't working, couldn't feel the usual burst of pixie dust in her chest and stomach like she usually did.

I need more. I have to have more.

She knew he would understand. He wouldn't be mad at her for needing him, for wanting him so bad. She would do anything for him, anything he wanted.

I can't take it. I'm coming back to you, my sweet Toad. I'm coming back to you and I don't ever want to leave you again.

She grabbed two handfuls of meat from the bed, felt hard bone poking her palm.

"You can't have me anymore. I'm all his now."

The balls of gore hit the wall and slapped to the floor, leaving splattered meaty patterns at the point of impact.

Jade laughed and touched herself as she imagined being back in Toad's presence, wrapping her body around his body, taking him in a mouthful at a time.

Kip could feel them coming back. And he wanted them back. But it would be different this time, he'd be more careful.

He couldn't let them feast on him anymore. He knew that now. As good as it felt, as much as he wanted to be a buffet for them, he didn't know if his body could take that again.

One person at a time, just a taste.

He could feel the pheromones twirling off his body like ghost fingers, beckoning his people back to him. And they were coming to him, he could feel them. Could taste them on the air.

Kip sat on the bottom stair, facing the door, and he smiled, stood, walked to the door and opened it before she had to knock.

"Hi, Jade. I'm glad you're back."

"You're not mad at me, right? I couldn't take it if you were mad at me." She was covered in blood, and though it was drying in places, it still glistened in the dying sunlight.

"I'm not mad." He pulled her in, embraced her, kissed her. Kip could tell from the smell that the blood coating her was not his or hers. He wrinkled his nose and backed away. "You need to wash that off. I don't like it."

Her face screwed up and she began to cry, crumbled into a ball of flesh at his feet. Nails scraped across the arches of his feet, across his toes.

"I'm sorry," she said. "I'll do anything you say. Just please…please let me taste you again."

Kip lifted back to her feet by her wrists, kissed her again. "Here." He popped a freshly filled pimple on his left cheekbone, left the exposed ball of pus on his face and leaned forward.

Jade cupped the back of his head, smashed her face against him, and snorted in her fix. She started to frenzy again, searching his skin for more, but Kip pulled away, shoved her back a few steps.

"That's enough. Now go wash up."

It looked like she wanted to protest, but just nodded, eyes going soft and dreamy as the pus took effect. A small smile pulled at her mouth, and she began exploring her sticky, red body with trembling fingers, shuddering with every breath.

"Go upstairs to the bathroom. Take a hot shower."

Jade nodded, tried to press her body to his, but he backed away, his heels hitting the bottom step. Jade looked hurt, but her hands still roamed her flesh, squeezed and massaged and fondled.

Kip stepped aside, pointed up the stairs, and she followed orders, was a good girl. Dried bloody footprints still stained the stairs from earlier in the day, when his entire flock had scattered. But as she ascended, she left fresh ones, wet and sparkling.

Kip took a long look at her ass, the way it bulged with each step. For a moment, the old Kip was back, and he couldn't believe he was staring at Jade Brewster's naked body in his home. And she was there for *him*, because she wanted *him* so bad. He could control her now. Had her in the palm of his hand. And though he was tempted to join her in the shower, finally get rid of the virginity that had accompanied him through life like some kind of imaginary friend, he decided to hold on to it. It didn't matter anymore. To fuck her would be so pointless now. He would be inside of her, was already inside of her, and no penetration could ever compare to that.

Another knock at the door. Kip had to force his eyes away from Jade's red breasts as she spun to face the noise. Jealousy twisted her mouth and pinched her eyes, but Kip scowled at her.

"Jade. Get in the shower. You don't want to make me mad, do you?"

She shook her head. "Never. But—"

"Jaaaade."

"Okay." She started to walk, then stopped momentarily. "I love you. I love you so bad."

"I know. Now go."

Kip strolled to the door, could hear them all out there, already starting to fight. He couldn't have that anymore either. Was sick of them fighting. They would behave themselves or get nothing.

He opened the door. They all hushed immediately and stared up at him, at their savior.

They started to rush toward him like some crazed stampede, but he held up a hand and stopped them in their tracks.

"Please, Kip. I'm begging you." Jezebel scratched at her wrists and forearms, the skin there already red from irritation. Her eyes bounced in all directions, puffy and pink from crying.

"I can't take it anymore. I'll…I'll fucking *kill* myself," Cash said as his knees hit the concrete of Kip's patio. The boy leaned forward, resting his forehead against Kip's feet.

There were at least six of them there now, and more were wandering toward the house from all directions. Each of them still wearing the dried blood from earlier in the day.

Kip lifted Cash to his feet, hugged him, patted him on the back.

"Please," Cash said, shaking his head. "I'm so sorry for how I treated you." His fist flew from his side and slammed into his own left eye.

Kip ruptured a zit on his forehead, motioned for Cash to take the custard. Cash squealed at the offering, eagerly sucked it up. The crowd grew restless, almost started shoving each other again, fighting, but Kip nudged Cash aside and glared at them. They didn't move.

"One at a time," Kip said. He felt powerful. He felt like a god.

But they didn't look ready to cooperate. Not like before. They looked desperate, and though Kip started to yell, started to let the anger take over like before, there was no stopping them.

Cash pounced on him from behind, pressed his mouth to the back of Kip's neck. Then the others were on him, no longer worried about Kip, only cared about feeding their need, their addiction. Like rabid, hungry dogs on a side of beef.

"No! I said no!"

But they weren't listening, were deaf to his shouting, his demands. He was on his back now, thrashing his arms and legs, twisting his face away from the mouths and teeth and tongues, but couldn't escape them.

And they sucked and drank and snorted him dry.

CHAPTER THIRTEEN

Zak found himself at the Grease Shack. He didn't know where else to go, and it was one of the only familiar places in town. He thought about just driving to school, sleeping in the parking lot, but the rumbling in his stomach brought him to the burger joint.

But once he got his cheeseburger and fries, he could only stare at it, the pangs in his belly becoming pure revulsion. The way the grease sparkled off the meat, the melted cheese running over the sides. The mayonnaise and ketchup overflowing from the soggy, soaked-through buns.

He tossed the food into the garbage, untouched, lit a cigarette and found an alternative rock station. He needed some noise to drown out the grotesque images running amok in his mind.

"Well, that was a waste."

Zak's stomach dropped at the sound of the voice, and he was sure it was going to be one of the kids from the house, one of Kip's addicts. He balled his hands into fists before cracking his eyes open, ready to defend himself. But then he relaxed when he saw her face.

"Gwendolyn?"

"Hey, he remembers my name. Too bad he didn't remember our tutoring session."

Zak didn't know what else to do but smile at her. It was the furthest thing from his mind, and even when he saw her, it didn't dawn on him until she had said something.

"Ah shit, Gwen. It's been a fucked up day...my head's all over the place. I'm sorry...I mean it. I didn't meant to—"

"Shut up already," she said and slugged him in the arm through the window. She wore a frown, but Zak could tell by her eyes that she wasn't really mad. "And did you just call me

Gwen? I just met you today, and you're already shortening my name?"

Zak shrugged, grinned. "Gwendolyn's a mouthful."

"Gwen it is then. So…can I join you? I mean, unless you're—"

"No. I mean…yes, you can join me. Please. I could use some friendly company right now."

As she rounded the car toward the passenger side, Zak flicked his cigarette away, quickly checked his breath and straightened his posture. She opened the door, sat down, ran her palms over her jeans.

"So…have you been here waiting all this time?" Zak said.

"Please. Get over yourself, man." Her cheeks burned bright red.

"Well…were you?"

She fingered a tear at the knee of her jeans, sort of snickered. Her eyes still hadn't left her lap since she had entered the car. "Well shit. What can I say?"

Zak laughed. "That's sweet. Now I really feel like shit."

"Look…I just felt bad for you. I mean, when it comes to math…you're kind of a retard." She finally looked at him. Her smile was perfect.

"No offense, but I'm not really in the mood for math."

"Me either. Can I ask what happened to your face? Wanna talk about it?"

Zak had completely forgotten about his injuries. He checked the mirror, winced as his tongue prodded at the tender opening on his lip. He was again reminded that it hurt to breathe, his ribs screaming in pain. His mind had been too busy to worry about his own beaten body.

"There's something weird going on," Zak said, turning in his seat so he was fully facing Gwen now. She did the same, looked like a little kid about to be read a bedtime story. "It's Kip. I don't know what the hell is going on…but it's scaring the shit out of me."

"Kip? As in your cousin? As in Toad?"

"Come on…out of everyone, I didn't think you'd call him that."

"I don't, I'm just saying. How can Kip scare you? He's a nice kid...but I can't imagine him scaring anyone."

Zak's vision went blurry as he stared off into space, thinking about the kids all over Kip, moaning and screaming and fucking and laughing. The way Kip bled and bled, the sound of his voice when he got angry.

He's a fucking monster.

"Zak?"

"Huh?"

"Lost you there for a second. Your mouth was moving but no words were coming out."

"Sorry." Zak focused his vision again, but when he locked eyes with Gwen, he had to force his stare into his lap. "It's his acne. It's...shit. I don't even know where to begin."

"His acne? I know it's bad, but why would you be scared of it?"

"Believe me...if you only knew the half of it, you'd be scared too. You wouldn't believe me if I told you. I promise you."

"Then show me."

"What?"

She smiled that perfect smile again, brushed her bangs out of her face. "Well, if Kip's in trouble, I'd like to help. I don't know him that well, but like I said, he's a good kid. I've always felt sorry for him, like it's my duty to be nice to him or something. I don't know. I'm a weirdo like that."

You're an angel is what you are.

"I don't think that's a good idea, Gwen. Trust me...you don't want to see this. Shit, I already saw it, and if I could, I would unsee the shit out of it. I don't even think I can make myself go back home."

She reached across the middle console and grabbed Zak's hand. When Zak locked eyes with her, she blushed, moved her eyes to their hands.

"I know I just met you, Zak. And believe me, I know how fucking corny this sounds." She rolled her eyes and snickered.

"Yeah? What is it?"

"Oh god, just... Let's just go. I want to help. Let me."

Zak wanted to tell her no, wanted to explain everything, but he couldn't find the words. He could only concentrate on her hand pressed against his, her thumb moving back and forth over his skin. Their eyes met again, neither of them looking away this time, staring deep into each other. And it felt good, it felt amazing. It felt right. Like nothing Zak had ever experienced with any other girl. He felt like he'd known this girl a lot longer than a day, and for whatever reason, he felt like he could trust her. Felt like she could handle the insanity that was Kip and his…condition.

"Okay. But I'm warning you. You won't believe it. Even as you're looking at it…at him. You won't believe it."

When her hand released his, he was filled with a strange sadness. He wanted to feel her touch again, wanted to reach over and hold her in his arms, press his mouth to hers.

But he put one hand on the steering wheel, the other on the shift. He reversed out of the Grease Shack's parking lot, then was heading back home. He still didn't know what he would do when they got there, and he couldn't shake the feeling that taking Gwendolyn there was a huge mistake, but if that's what she wanted, he'd let her see.

If anyone can convince Kip to get help, maybe it's her.

It wasn't until the child's legs stopped kicking that Chuck realized he'd done a bad thing. He stood, staring down at the broken, tiny body. His jaw ached from clenching his teeth.

He recognized this boy. *Chelsea's brother? Where the fuck am I?*

It came back all at once, and he remembered what he did, almost felt bad about it until his need kicked in again, stronger than ever. He tried to calm the shakes by licking Toad's dried blood off his skin, but it wasn't enough, didn't satisfy him.

He moved away from the boy, who was bent nearly in half. Blood still leaked from his body, but slowly. Another burst of panic set in, and he hated himself for hurting the boy, for hurting Chelsea's brother…

Chelsea!

He ran back to her room, collapsed beside her body. Tears

and saliva dripped from his face, soaked into the gaping wound of her mouth. Chuck rested his forehead against hers, wept, held her hand in his.

But as her cold flesh touched him, he realized it wasn't because of her he was filled with such abyssal sadness. It was because of the absence of Kip. If he could just be with Toad again, everything would be okay, everything would be perfect.

Now he remembered perfectly well. Chelsea had been trying to take it from him. That's what she did. Her family too. They all got what they deserved.

Chuck stood, stomped on Chelsea's split head with his heel, as hard as he could. Meat squished and bone cracked, and he kept pounding down on her, screaming, muscles aching from being so tight and tense.

A weak moan floated into the room from somewhere in the house. Chuck ran toward the noise, stormed down the stairs until he found the woman. Her crooked legs were being dragged behind her and she clawed at the ground. When she saw Chuck, a scream exploded from her throat.

A man lay on his back, his head cracked open like an egg. Gray meat oozed out, and there was so much blood. But he wasn't moving, wasn't screaming. So it was the woman Chuck went after, lifted her into the air with ease. She was small, light, could barely fight back.

When her body left the ground, she made a series of gurgling and coughing sounds, as if she was trying to scream but couldn't get it past the blood in her throat.

Chuck walked her across the room toward the wall by the front door, roared as he threw her against it. Her body slammed into it, hit the ground hard. She gasped, groaned, writhed slightly. Chuck bounded toward her broken form, grabbed both ankles, spun until her body hovered over the ground, then slammed it into the wall again, painting it red where her face smacked it.

She stopped moving then. Stopped making any sounds at all.

"The Toad is mine!" When he said it this time, his voice shook, the need making him weak.

He was out the door and sprinting down the street then. The sun was gone. The night sky was littered with gray feathered clouds and the air smelled electric.

Chuck's body throbbed with withdrawal, but it only made his legs pump faster, working double time to get him back to Toad's place where he could beg for another hit. Anything. Just something.

I'll suck his dick if he wants me too. I bet his cum is just as good as his pus and blood...

It didn't take him long to get there. The closer he got to Kip's house, the more powerful his need became. It was like the house itself was radiating heat, and by the time Chuck stood in the front yard, staring at the kids as they feasted on Toad's motionless body on the porch, he felt completely engulfed in flame.

A few of the kids lay in the grass, giggling, rolling around and touching themselves. The first boy that Chuck ran up to caught Chuck's foot to the middle of his face.

Stomp stomp stomp.

They started to run away then, as if they had had enough. As if they had reached their peak and no longer needed Toad. Which meant there was nothing left for Chuck.

Most fled at the sight of Chuck rampaging toward them, cackling into the night as they scattered in all directions. Those too fucked up to move off the lawn were pummeled out of frustration, but were numb to their own pain, and they eventually joined the others and disappeared into the blackness surrounding them.

Only Jade remained. She held Toad's head in her lap, sucking on his forehead, but she sobbed, shoved the boy's head away and buried her face in her palms.

Toad wasn't moving, didn't look like he was breathing. His skin had taken on a purple, almost blue color. His eyes were completely white, rimmed with a neon green, that same green ringed around each nostril and at the corners of his mouth.

"There's nothing left," Jade said and shoved Kip's body completely out of her lap.

"But...but there has to be. I need him."

Jade paced the front porch, then started slamming her forehead into the door, again and again, muttering something that Chuck couldn't decipher.

Chuck ran his hands over Kip's body, looking for any bumps the others might have missed, but they were all craters now. And no blood ran out of them. Some blood stained the concrete, and Chuck quickly ran his tongue across the rough surface, hard enough to strip layers of skin, but he kept licking, desperate for any taste at all.

Then he smelled it. He wasn't sure how Jade could have missed it. Or maybe she was too fucking stupid to realize. Chuck wanted any part of Toad. Anything.

It seemed that at some point in his struggle, Kip had shit himself. Maybe it was like Chuck had heard—he couldn't remember where—that people shit their pants right after they die. He couldn't tell if Kip was dead or not, but the scent of shit was heavy in the air, and though it didn't spark his addiction, he knew it would work. It would work just like the pus and blood.

Chuck looked up and Jade was still slamming her head against the door, crying and screaming. There was another quick spark of the old Chuck, just quick enough for him to remember how much he loved Jade, how badly he wanted to be with her. He had an urge to scoop her up in his arms, keep her from hurting herself, take her away with him where they could be together and share the last offering the Toad would ever give.

And now Chelsea is gone. Out of the picture. It can just be me and Jade, forever, just like I always wanted.

But now...he didn't want that. He only wanted to be alone with his fix, just him and Toad's shit. Somewhere secret, where nobody would find him, where nobody could try and take his prize away from him.

He shot one last look at Jade, and she seemed completely oblivious of his presence. His eyes drank in her body, and his groin stirred, fluttered once, but remained flaccid. He had other things to worry about, more pressing things.

Kip's pants had already been torn, his boxer shorts already pulled down to the get at the forest of acne on his ass cheeks. But globs of dark shit lay in the seat of the underwear. Chuck took hold of the soiled fabric, ripped it free of the body. When the light hit it, iridescent colors rainbowed across the surface of the feces. Greens and purples and pinks and yellows.

It's mine…it's all mine.

Chuck wanted to do something to help Kip, only because if the kid died, Chuck knew he would die right along with him. Without Kip's secretions, Chuck didn't know how he would live through the night.

He checked in every direction. Nobody was there. Then there were headlights, growing brighter and brighter, and before the car could get any closer, Chuck tucked the warm shorts under his arm and sprinted into the night, heading straight for the trees.

"Is that…is that Chuck?" Gwen had both hands on the dashboard, peering out through the windshield.

Chuck was naked, looked completely covered in blood. He held something, looked like some kind of clothing, but as soon as Zak pulled up, Chuck took off. Zak lost sight of him almost instantly, but didn't bother trying to chase him.

"That's fucking Kip…oh shit… *Oh god!*" Zak fumbled with his door handle, his hands shaking uncontrollably.

Kip lay on the porch, completely still, his body riddled with wounds. The same type of wounds as before, like empty eye sockets, but this time there was no blood. But the wounds looked fresh, glistened like raw chicken. Kip wasn't moving at all, not even the up and down of his stomach to show he was breathing. His skin looked awful, a strange purplish blue color, not the pale color of someone suffering from massive blood loss.

"What the fuck did you do!" Zak grabbed Jade by the shoulders, spun her around. The tips of his fingers dug into the meat of her arms, but she could only sob, her dilated eyes streaming an endless torrent of tears.

"He's dried up," she said through her violent weeps.

Ropes of thick saliva connected her lips like harp strings. "I need him, Zak. Do something. *You have to fix him!*"

"Zak...we need to get him to the hospital. Like...now," Gwen said from behind him, placing a soft hand on his shoulder.

Zak growled and threw Jade backward and away from Kip as hard as he could. Jade hit the door, her blood-stained breasts jiggling, then dropped to her knees, continued to weep.

Zak could only imagine what was going through Gwen's mind right then. He wanted to turn to her, explain, but there wasn't time. He cradled Kip's body in his arms—it was so light. The skin felt hot to the touch. Zak figured that had to be a good sign. A dead body would be cold, especially on a cool night like this.

Turning toward his Corolla, Zak carried Kip's body across the lawn. Gwen jogged beside him, staring at Kip's face and torso with wide eyes and a furrowed brow, her head slightly shaking. She threw the back passenger door open.

"What's wrong with his skin? Why is it that color? And why the hell is Jade Brewster here, naked and covered in blood? And Chuck?"

"I told you...everything is fucked up. But his skin...it wasn't this color before. I don't know what's—"

Zak was just about to place his cousin into the back seat when Kip's eyes burst open.

It surprised Zak, induced a scream, and he nearly dropped Kip. Once Kip's skin got to moving again, thrashing and bubbling, Zak did drop him, backed away.

Kip hit the lawn with a thud, and Gwen started to rush toward him, but Zak caught her by the arm and pulled her away. She struggled for a few seconds until she caught sight of the pulsating skin, the empty wounds filling with pus before their eyes, but it was a creamy purple color, the boils the color of blueberries as they bulged fatter and fatter.

"Zak...what's wrong with him? His skin...oh my god..."

"Toad!" Jade sprinted across the lawn, bumping into Gwen as she passed and knocking her over. "Oh my god,

baby…I was so scared. I thought…I thought you left me. Don't you ever leave me, not evereverever!"

Kip stood, the blue and purple boils still thumping, and he smiled at Zak. Even his teeth seemed to have a blue tint, his eyes twitchy and rimmed in a neon green color. His skin sparkled in the moonlight as the juices flowed and rejuvenated him, each open wound now a pustule filled to bursting with that purple substance.

"Zak," Kip said, eyes blinking one at a time, pupils vibrating. His voice was deeper, almost like a growl. His smile took up half his face, green at the corners, his lips split down the middle to allow the smile to stretch further. The gums looked black, his tongue the same. "My cousin. Where have you been?"

Jade held Kip tight, rubbed her tits and groin over his left side, humping him like some horny dog, whimpering and moaning, begging him.

But Kip ignored her completely. Because his eyes were now locked on Gwendolyn.

Gwen just stared at the scene unfolding before her, jaw hanging, head shaking.

Zak quickly helped Gwen to her feet, shot a nervous glance toward Kip. He didn't need his cousin getting jealous. His heart pounded in his chest, made it hard to breathe.

Kip's eyes were still locked on Gwen, and when he loosened his smile, black blood oozed from his cracked lips, dripped from his chin. Jade thrust her head forward as if to drink it up, but Kip caught her by the throat, pushed her away, then finally let his eyes roll back to Zak.

Kip's stare was hard, accusatory, pupils still shaking and rattling. His green-encrusted nostrils widened, and he took a long step forward. His flesh had slowed now, and his body looked swollen, infected. He had a stench like insecticide.

And then he smiled again. His eyes stayed hard, but his mouth pulled tight across his face.

"Zak, I see you've met Gwendolyn. Hi, Gwendolyn. Remember my cousin I was telling you about? Isn't he fucking dreamy?"

"Whoa whoa," Zak said. "She came here because she was worried about you, Kip. I thought maybe she could help, so—"

"Yes, always worried about me. Always felt sorry for me. Isn't that right, Gwendolyn? Never a shortage of pity for the Toad, yeah?"

"Kip, w-what's wrong with you? What happened?" Gwen stepped forward, but quickly took a step back when Kip approached her.

"It's the same old thing, Gwendolyn. I thought things would be different now. I thought they wanted me. Thought they needed me. But they don't want me. They don't give a fuck about me. Never did before, and they don't now. It's what's *inside* of me they want."

Zak knew Gwen must have been beyond confused, and he now wished he would have filled her in, regardless of how ridiculous it all sounded. But he didn't expect this. Zak wondered if the monster inside of Kip was surfacing more and more, slowly eating away at the old Kip, taking over him. The thing in front of him was not his cousin.

"Kip, listen to me." Gwen took a deep breath, reached out and took Kip's hand. She only hesitated for a second before grabbing it, and Zak wanted so bad to pull her away, get Kip's purplish, pus-filled skin away from hers.

Kip's expression softened then, and he blinked rapidly as he stared down at his hand in Gwen's. For a second, he looked like himself, scared and shy, a boy with a crush.

Jade screamed on the ground, tearing out fistfuls of grass and dirt and flinging it all around. She bared her teeth as she stared at Gwen holding hands with Kip, and Zak stayed on the defensive in case she tried anything.

"You're better than all those fucking assholes at school. You should know that. Five years from now, all those popular dipshits will be fucking worthless, probably bagging your groceries or stirring milkshakes. But you? You've got great things ahead of you. Don't let all this high school bullshit get to your head."

Kip's chin dipped until it touched his chest. When

his shoulders started jumping, Zak thought he was crying, thought that maybe Gwen had somehow gotten to him, that maybe Kip would snap out of it and be the kid Zak grew up with again. His best friend again. The kid that loved comic books and video games and shitty horror movies.

But Kip was laughing. The laugh grew in volume until it became a cackle, and he leaned his head back and howled at the moon. His hand clenched around Gwen's, and she tried to pull it away, shot Zak a quick glance that begged for help.

"Kip, let her go, man. What the fuck is wrong with you?"

Kip's laugh was cut off at once, and his head snapped forward so fast, a splash of purple pus erupted from his face into the dirt, narrowly missing Gwen.

"What's wrong with me, cousin? I'm all alone. Just like I've always been. I thought at least I had you. My own fucking cousin, my flesh and blood. But even you betrayed me."

"Betrayed you? You've got it all wrong, Kip. Please."

"Let me go!" Gwen balled her hand into a fist and swung, catching Kip on the chin and making him stumble back. His hand slipped free of Gwen's, and she stared at the iridescent mucus coating her knuckles, gagged.

"You see? She thinks I'm fucking disgusting! She always did!" Kip held his hand out for Jade, and she gladly took it, was hauled to her feet. Kip pulled her in and kissed her, made sure both of their tongues were visible for Zak and Gwen. He squeezed her breasts, her ass, then smiled wider than ever.

"I love you, Toad," Jade said, her voice low and trembling.

"I know you do. Why don't we go inside? I want to show you something."

With her hand still in his, Kip led Jade across the lawn and back toward the house. He slapped her on the ass just as they passed over the threshold, then Kip turned back around to face Zak and Gwen.

"You know what, cousin? I think maybe I *will* have a party. Invite all my new friends over, yeah? It'll be a fucking blast, won't it?"

Kip widened his eyes and let his grin stretch tight again, then slammed the door.

Zak fought the urge to run into the house. He swung his fists through the air, clenching his teeth. "Fuck! *Motherfucker!*"

"Zak...what are we gonna do? Jesus Christ...tell me what's happening here."

Zak took a deep breath, ushered Gwen back into his car, then peeled off.

"Where are we going?"

"The police station. Fuck this, I'm not doing this shit anymore. He needs help. I'll tell them to bring an ambulance too."

"But what the fuck is going on!"

Zak sighed through his nostrils. "So it was Senior Skip Day..."

CHAPTER FOURTEEN

Kip led Jade straight up the attic stairs into his bedroom. She kept trying to get to Kip's skin, and every time Kip would push her away and refuse her, she would pout, bare her teeth, squeal in frustration.

"Just be patient. You'll get more. You'll get more than you'll ever need."

"Oh, Toad, baby. Fuck...I love you so much. I just fucking love you so much..."

Lies. All fucking lies! You don't love me. Nobody fucking loves me!

But Kip just smiled, kissed her.

He felt different now. Strong. Venomous. Like there was acid pumping through his veins. He couldn't feel his body anymore. No more orgasmic pulsating. Everything was just numb now, yet he could feel the heat, could feel the new juices flowing through him.

He knew what he had to do. And they deserved it. Every fucking one of them.

And Zak too. He knew I loved her. He fucking knew...but he has to have everything for himself. He just couldn't stand that I was the popular one now...couldn't stand that Kip was getting his time in the sun. No. And he can die with the rest of them.

"Come here, Jade."

She obeyed.

Kip sat on his bed. He realized for the first time since waking back up again, since becoming this new being, a new entity all together, that he was completely nude. His cock was limp, covered in purple and blue boils that swirled with fresh pus. But not like the pus from before. He could tell, deep inside, that something had changed. His body was done

135

making others feel good. They had abused it, forced his body to transform, to go into defensive mode. Self-preservation.

The pus was liquid hate. It was all the years Kip had been made fun of, all the years he had been ridiculed and embarrassed. No friends, no girls. Years of feeling worthless and grotesque. All of those feelings had become a physical thing, a poisonous liquid, and it continued to swell his flesh all over his body.

"You want me to suck your cock, baby? I'll suck it so good. Please let me…please." Jade said the words as she ogled the bumps on the head and shaft of his still-flaccid penis. Her hand darted out and she rubbed it, her tight grip bursting some of the bumps there.

Purple and blue and green fluid oozed out, as thick and viscous as maple syrup.

And she leaned over and took it into her mouth, sucked and sucked, bobbing her head.

Kip could feel nothing, but he stared down at the top of her head and smiled, his phlegmy laugh rattling at the back of his throat.

Jade moaned deep, her fingernails digging into Kip's thighs as she slurped up the juices, letting his puffy, soft shaft slide across her lips.

It started at the top of her head. At least that was Kip's point of view.

Her scalp turned hot pink, the hair falling out in clumps. The flesh bubbled, liquefied, spilled from her head onto Kip's lap.

She choked, started to hyperventilate, tried to push away from him, but Kip reached out, grabbed her head with both hands, and continued to fuck her mouth with his loose cock.

The flesh on either side of her head, where Kip held her, started to slide off in sloppy chunks, and he finally released her, tossed her to the floor where he could watch.

Purples and blues and greens and yellows. Her liquefied innards spilled from her melting skin in rainbow colors, bubbled on the ground like hot grease. Steam swirled off the soupy mess, filled the air with the smell of hate and vengeance.

Even her bones melted, like sticks of butter, but she still moved slightly, still clung to some shred of life. Her mouth worked up and down as if she were trying to speak, even though her mouth was filled with the liquefied meat of her tongue and gums. Her face was little more than a pink and purple skull that was already beginning to collapse in on itself.

Kip stood, clapped as he watched the rest of her dissolve into a pile of brilliant color.

Yes, it was time for a party. And Kip couldn't wait for the festivities to begin.

He strolled down the attic steps, whistling as he went, walked back outside, and stood in his front yard.

His body called to them.

And when they arrived, he would give them what they wanted. He would give each and every one of them what they deserved.

Chuck sat Indian-style in the woods. It was a spot that Jade had showed him a few months ago. They had skipped school and she directed him to drive his Mustang through the trees into a clearing where they fucked liked rabbits again and again. Chuck remembered how sore his dick was the next day.

But now Jade was with Kip. And Chuck was glad. Whatever made Kip happy made Chuck happy.

But he's dead now. He's dead and this is all that's left of him.

Chuck held up the torn underwear, let the moonlight illuminate the chunky smear. Again, as the light danced over the shit's surface, it dazzled with color, as if Kip's last meal had been a bowl of multi-colored glitter.

Chuck licked his lips, his hands shaking now because of how bad he needed the Toad. Every cell in his body begged him to stuff that shit into his mouth and swallow it, make all the pain melt away.

What am I doing? I can't eat shit…what the fuck is wrong with me?

Chuck didn't know where that thought came from, but he laughed it off, ran his teeth over the fabric and scraped the feces into his mouth. The taste wasn't what he had expected. There was some spiciness to it, with a hint of sweetness. He chewed it, let it soak into his palette and tongue, and then finally swallowed.

He ran his tongue over the boxer shorts, making sure he got every bit, didn't want to waste a single morsel.

It started in his gut. At first, it was the same feeling he had been craving, and he jumped to his feet and tittered as the soothing vibrations snaked through his entrails. But that only lasted a few seconds. The smile on his face twisted into a knot of confusion and agony as it felt like a barbed balloon was blowing up in his belly, getting bigger and bigger, the needles growing longer and sharper.

He clutched his stomach and fell to his knees, black liquid streaming from his throat and turning the dirt below him into mud.

What's happening to me? What...what the fuck?

He tried to clench his teeth, but they mushed into his gums and began to fall out one by one. Another gout of black ink roared from his mouth, followed by a scream that felt encrusted in broken glass.

The searing pain traveled from his gut up into his throat, building speed as it went, leaving a trail of fire behind. Once it reached his head, Chuck was flopping around in the dirt, no longer capable of screaming, no longer capable of thinking.

It was as if the shit had crawled itself into his skull, ate his brain, and was now doing his thinking for him.

Chuck rolled over onto his back, stared up at the sky. The black of the night had been transformed into streaks of vibrating and pulsating color, like an orgy of rainbows.

Chuck smiled. At least he thought he smiled. Something hot and chunky kept spilling from his mouth, running from his nostrils. It wasn't until he stood that he realized his stomach had blown out and that his innards hung from the gaping cave like giant squid tentacles.

He laughed, poked and prodded at the fleshy tubes. Pain

erupted there, but it was a different kind of pain, an almost ticklish, silly pain.

The ground moved, looked like a sea of rotting flesh, and every time he took a step, his foot plunged into the rancid meat and maggots wiggled out and danced over his feet.

The trees looked like giant corpses, hanging over him, promising him death and torture, so he climbed one of them, his intestines snagging and ripping open on branches as he went. He found the thickest limb he could, wrapped both hands around it, then hung from it, bouncing his body weight until it snapped free and he went tumbling back to the sea of rot beneath him.

The limb bled in his hands, and he gave it a few test swings.

"Killkillkillkillkill. Blood and pus and shit and *everyone will fucking die!*"

He didn't mean to say anything, the words just sort of spilled out of his mouth, hot and salty. But in his mind, it made perfect sense. He knew what he had to do. It's what Toad would have wanted him to do. Make them suffer.

Everyone must suffer.

And then he felt it. As if the sky had opened up and was raining cactus needles.

Toad is alive. And he's calling for me.

Chuck bounded through the woods, following the directions that echoed through his shattered mind.

"Ho. Lee. Shit." Gwen blew air from her tight lips as she ran both hands through her hair. She shot Zak a look, slightly smirking, as if she were waiting for him to tell her he was joking.

But Zak kept a straight face, was doing everything he could not to cry in front of her.

"That's just…that's more fucked up than anything should be allowed to be. I mean…fuck, man."

"Yeah. Exactly. I still don't believe it's happening, but there's no denying it now. The shit is real, and it's my fucking cousin it's happening to." Zak slammed his palms against the steering wheel, honking the horn. "Why him? Why Kip? There are so many more fucking assholes in this world, in this fucking town, that deserves it more than him. He's been nothing but good his whole life…and now this?"

"I always thought he had the worst case of acne I've ever seen. But…wow. Just wow."

Zak didn't know how he expected Gwen to react, but her tone was pissing him off.

"So what now? Are you really going to tell that story to the police?"

"No, of course not. I'll just tell them…fuck, I don't know. I'll tell them Kip might be dangerous, you know? Like Columbine dangerous. They'll sure as fuck listen then."

She scrunched her brow, and for a minute, Zak thought she was going to protest, but she just nodded. "Yeah. That's pretty smart actually. Then when they get to the house, we won't have to tell them anything, they'll see it for themselves, right?"

"Exactly."

They were silent for a few minutes, both seeming to marinate in their own deep thoughts. Then Gwen wrinkled her nose, stuck out her tongue, and wiggled like she had a tingle in her spine.

"They actually ate his pus? Jesus that's so fucked up. But you know what?" She smiled, raised an eyebrow, glared out the windshield with blank eyes. "They all deserved it. For treating him like shit for so long."

"They deserved to have their asses kicked, yes. But this? I don't think anyone deserves this. And you know what's fucked up? I wasn't gonna tell you this…"

"What? What is it?"

"I felt it too. I wanted to suck his pus down just like everyone else. I think his body releases something into the air, makes the people around him crave it. Or maybe it's just fucked up people like me and all those other fucking kids."

"Did you…did you eat—"

"No! Hell no. I could feel the craving, but I fought it off. It woke up some feelings that I've been working really hard to bury, though. Even now I can kind of feel it. And it pisses me off."

"There!" Gwen pointed out the window with one hand, slapped Zak on the shoulder with the other.

"What?"

"There, right fucking there."

The police car was parked at a Seven Eleven, the officer sipping coffee and leaning against the vehicle, absently fiddling with his cell phone.

Zak nearly zoomed right past the gas station, but swung the wheel to the left, cutting across traffic and nearly getting t-boned by a minivan. He pulled the car into the parking lot, the officer already approaching the car, one hand resting on his sidearm.

"Don't start screaming at him, Zak. Be calm."

"Yeah...okay." Zak rolled the window down.

"Get out of the car, son." The officer squinted at him, then knelt down so he could get a look at Gwen.

Zak didn't resist, got out, hands up. "I'm sorry, sir. We saw you standing here and we really need to talk with you. I didn't mean to—"

"You could have killed somebody with a stunt like that. Are you crazy?"

"I know, and I'm sorry, sir. But there's something way more serious going on. And it's time sensitive. People could be in danger. Kids."

"How much you had to drink today, son? And be honest with me." Still squinting.

"Drink? Nothing. I panicked, that's all."

"Step over here, please. Arms out."

Zak shot a quick look at Gwen and she widened her eyes, nodded toward the officer. Zak sighed, went along with the entire sobriety test. When he passed, he was about ready to scream. He had no idea how much time had passed, but it felt like a lifetime.

"Be more careful, you hear me? Now go on."

"Go on? Did you not hear what I said? People are in trouble, high school kids could be dead before tonight is over."

"Dead?"

Zak laid out the whole lie. Just sort of made it up as he went, making sure to make it sound serious so the officer would listen.

"And I don't know how to make bombs, but it sure looks like he's stockpiling a whole lot of chemicals and serious-looking equipment. He's been bullied his whole life, and I'm scared he's finally had enough. I'm scared he's going to do something bad tonight. I need you to come to the house. You can follow me there."

The officer scratched his chin, face as red as diaper rash. When he nodded, Zak almost hugged him.

"Tell you what…let me call this in, get some backup just in case. If what you're telling me is true, I don't want to be there alone." The officer smiled, placed a hard hand on Zak's shoulder. "I know it's hard to turn in your cousin like this, but you did—"

Something warm and wet splashed Zak in the face at the same moment Gwen shrieked.

Zak didn't know what he was looking at at first. The officer's hand dropped to his side, and he sort of blinked, mouth opening and closing. Something big had been smashed into the top of his head, and it wasn't until the officer dropped to his knees that Zak saw Chuck standing there, the blood that had been covering his body earlier now a flaky red crust. It looked like his stomach had been blown out from the inside, flaps of skin hanging off in tattered ribbons, and his intestines dragged on the concrete in torn loops.

The officer was hurt, but still conscious. He tried to stand, tried to pull out his gun, but Chuck swung the thick tree branch over his head, smashed it back down onto the officer's skull. Then again. And when he did it a fourth time, the officer's head dented inward, blood bubbling out of the wound and trickling from his ears.

Chuck held his weapon above his head with both hands, looked like a cavemen doing a victory dance after bagging a meal. His intestines bounced and splashed black liquid everywhere.

"Rotten. It's all rotten and the rainbows will fuck the night away!"

"What?" Zak backed away from the crazed jock.

Chuck grinned, his eyes pointing in opposite directions like a chameleon. His teeth were black, lips caked in a crusty dark gray substance. Then he cocked back his branch and swung.

Zak ducked it just in time and the wood shattered the driver's window of his Corolla. Gwen screamed again.

Chuck peered into the car, grabbed hold of his dick when he saw Gwen, and started stroking. He made a choking, gurgled sound, and a waterfall of inky black liquid rushed from his mouth poured all over his hand and cock, and he just kept pumping away, didn't let the endless black vomit stream slow him.

Zak figured Chuck must have got a hold of more of Toad's pus, either that or he was losing his mind from withdrawal. The guy looked like he had been self-mutilating since they last saw him jogging away from the house, and Zak figured Chuck would be dead from his wounds before long.

But he didn't have time to wait for that to happen.

Chuck was leaning into the driver's window, reaching for Gwen. She finally stopped screaming and ran out of her door and across the parking lot. Chuck pulled himself out, cackled, pointed at her with his tree limb.

"Can you feel it? Can you feel the Toad's fingers on your cunt?" Chuck shoved a fist into his stomach cavity, pushed it in and out of the bramble of innards there. "I can feel him right in my cunt too. He's calling us. *He's calling us!*"

"What in the hell is going on out here?" The gas station attendant stood just in front of the double glass doors, the yellow and red light from the sign making him look orange. He pointed a shaking pistol at Chuck, eyes kept bouncing to the dead officer and the growing puddle of blood creeping from his head.

"Kill them all. Everyone must suffer. They all deserve it, they all deserve to *fucking die!*" As Chuck ran toward the man, another stream of black shot from his mouth and misted behind him as he went, tree limb held high.

"Stop! *Don't come any closer!* I already called the police and they're coming!"

"Fucking shoot him!" Gwen screamed.

And the man did. He fired the gun twice, both shots hitting Chuck in the guts as far as Zak could tell, but it didn't even slow the rampaging jock down.

The wood slammed into the top of the man's head, dropping him face-first into the pavement.

"Chuck! *Stop it!*" Zak held both hands in the air, approaching the kid slow and steady. "Kip doesn't want this. Okay? Don't do this."

Chuck turned, his mouth, guts, and genitals all tattooed that black color. His eyes sort of circled in place, never once facing the same direction. A stupid chuckle sputtered from his lips, and he turned back to the attendant, raised his weapon high, and slammed it back down.

This man's head gave quicker than the officer's. His legs kicked, the toes of his shoes tapping against the concrete, hand slapping with the same chaotic motion.

Chuck hit him again until the back of his head was a mess of broken skull, hair, and brain matter. Chuck's punched his fist into the opening, scooped out a handful of gray meat, then he shoved it into his own stomach cavity.

"I think I'm hungry," Chuck said, then roared with laughter before sprinting toward Zak, nearly tripping over his viscera.

How is this motherfucker still standing?

The gun went off just beside him, and Zak fell to the ground and covered himself up. There were five more shots that rang out, and Chuck's body hit the concrete, the exit wounds in the back of his head bubbling black liquid.

Zak looked up at Gwen, the officer's pistol in her hands, smoke spiraling from the barrel.

"Fucking cocksucker," she said. Her lips were tight and pinched shut, nostrils flaring, tears slowly falling from her slow blinking eyes.

Zak jumped to his feet, knees shaking. "Did you hear

what he said?"

"Not a single fucking thing he said made a damn bit of sense. It was all gibberish, right? Like he went fucking cuckoo."

"Most of it, yeah. But he said something about Toad calling him, calling everyone."

"What does it mean?" Gwen still had the gun pointed at Chuck's body, that black stuff still flowing from his wounds.

"Remember how I told you about that chemical? They're like pheromones I think. If Chuck could sense them way the fuck out here..."

"Kip did say he was going to have a party. Right before we left."

"Fuck me. Something's changed, Gwen. Before...they were like addicts, right? Like they were all on ultra-potent ecstasy or something. Not like this though. And Kip had changed too...the color of his skin, the way he looked all bloated. Something's changing, and if we don't stop this shit now, I have a feeling Bowie High School's gonna have one hell of a small graduating class."

"What about the cops? Shouldn't we call them?"

Zak wanted to, was terrified to face his cousin alone. "After all this shit? They'll have questions, and we don't have time for questions. Besides..."

"What?"

"I don't want Kip to get hurt. Not if we don't have to. I still love him...he's still my cousin."

Zak expected Gwen to call him crazy, but she just arched her mouth, nodded. "I understand."

A pickup truck pulled into the parking lot then, an elderly man at the wheel. When he caught sight of all the violence, he immediately picked up his cell phone and started dialing. Then he saw Zak and Gwen, pointed an accusatory finger, and started shouting into his phone.

"Let's get the fuck out of here. If we're not already too late."

Gwen kept the gun, and Zak still had his pistol in his glove compartment. He hoped to god they wouldn't need them.

CHAPTER FIFTEEN

They came. Just like he knew they would. His power to call them to him had only intensified since his rebirth. Now they were completely powerless to resist him, no matter where they were, no matter how far away.

And that's exactly what it was: a rebirth. He understood that as soon as consciousness had brought him back out of the darkness. It had been just like before at first. He had been swimming through an abyss of nothing, pain erupting all over his body as his followers drank him up, dried him out. The pain was there, just like last time, but it was quickly replaced with something else. Something that pumped through his body as blood once did.

Hate. Pure, poisonous hate.

His flesh became the hate, was soaked to the bone in it. He sprouted new boils all over his body, covering every part of him now, each one of them bulging with the new lethal fluid.

Kip thought he had it all figured out too. Before, all he wanted was to make friends. He wanted the other kids to stop being disgusted by him and accept him as one of them, an equal. He wanted the opposite sex to desire him, to want him and swoon over him the way they did to guys like Chuck and Zak. And so his flesh spits out pus and blood with the ability to make the things Kip wanted a reality. He doesn't know why or how, but that's what it was. But now. Now he no longer wanted these things. Now he only wanted them to pay, each and every one of them. He wanted them to suffer, to feel what it feels like to be treated like you are less than human, like some kind of freak.

He wanted them all dead. Reduced to shit.

And his flesh now gave him the ability to do just that.

Kip stood in his room, staring at his reflection, unable to

stop smiling. He used to glare at the mirror full of trepidation. Scared every day to go to school and face the other kids looking the way he did. He hated his appearance. Even though his acne was so pleasurable, it was still the cause of being an outsider, of being alienated from his entire class. He'd spent many a night crying as he looked at himself, wishing he could be someone else. Anyone else. Anyone but Toad.

But now?

Now he could see his true beauty. He could see that he was perfect.

They called to him, screaming and roaring for his pus, his blood. They cursed at each other, sounded like they were tearing each other apart down there. Kip had given them instructions to stay on the first floor and wait for him.

And they obeyed, though they weren't happy about it. To delay their feeding another second was pure agony for them.

Kip stared at the vibrant puddle that was once Jade. Smoke still danced off the liquid, bubbling and hissing as it ate at the wood floor.

Soon, they would all be reduced to this. And Kip would swim in them. He'd engulf himself in their liquefied flesh and bone, drown in it.

He ran his fingers over his torso, his belly. His fingertips caressed his cheeks, forehead, chin. The acne begged to be opened up, begged to be drained. His entire body pulsated, and he knew it was time.

The attic steps were lowered, and Kip slowly made his way down. Then he made his way to the top of the stairway, stared down at all the kids as they argued and fought. Cussing and punching and kicking and biting. All of them claiming Toad as their own. None wanting to share his fluids.

Kip said nothing as he began his descent. Once the first set of eyes landed on him, the rest followed. All argument and ruckus quickly cut off then, each of them staring up at Kip like he was a girl on her prom night, showing her dress for the first time.

"Toad...oh god. *I need you so fucking bad!*"

"Please...oh please..."

Kip raised a hand to stop all talking. He didn't have to say a word for them to understand. The only sound was his footsteps as he slowly took the steps down toward his addicts. As he grew closer, step by soft, spongy step, tongues darted out to wet lips, hands rubbed against each other, nails were raked across flesh.

Black blood and multi-colored pus rained from his body and pitter-pattered onto the steps. It was as if his flesh was completely filled, a sponge soaked to capacity.

Once he reached the first floor, they parted, almost as if they could sense danger, could sense that something was different than before. Faces twisted in disgust, and they resembled themselves before ever getting a taste of what lay within Kip's skin. For a few seconds, they were the same kids they used to be, the same kids that would only talk to Kip to make fun of him, to make themselves feel better by making him feel like dog shit.

In those brief seconds, Kip panicked. Could feel his old self rising from the pus swamp within his mind, terrified of these people. All he wanted to do was hide in his room like he used to, curl up on his bed and cower.

But then their need, their addiction, took over again. Tongues basted lips, eyes widened. They began to close in.

Kip grinned, held his arms out, spread his legs, lifted his chin.

And they came to him. Lips and teeth and tongues. Hands and fingers and nails. Sucking and slurping and sipping and moaning. Most were too excited, too blinded by their own need that they couldn't even tell their bodies were beginning to bubble, flesh sloughing off in huge sloppy chunks. Skin split, showed the red muscle and white bone beneath.

The screams started then. Mouths detached, teeth unclamped. The screams only lasted a few seconds before their throats were filled with their soupy innards pushing past their tongues to splash onto the floor.

Purples and greens oozed as the flesh melted, mixed with yellows and pinks and blues. Kip stretched his mouth as wide as it would go and cackled.

His fellow students thrashed on the floor in front of him, colliding with each other as they groaned and gurgled. The tile glistened with their fluids.

Then Kip heard a slight whimper, coming from behind him. He turned, smiled, reached out and ran his bloated, throbbing fingers through the boy's hair. It was Cash, one of Chuck's buddies. The boy's flesh had begun to run, to spill off of him, but slower than the others. Must have noticed what was happening and unlatched before he could ingest too much of Kip's new and improved pus.

Kip used his teeth, opened up a gash on his left forearm. The blood was pure black, and it oozed out quickly, splashed over the floor and onto the writhing mess that had once been the popular kids of Bowie High.

Cash shook his head, looked like he was trying to say something, but couldn't get any words past his swollen, bubbling throat.

"What's the matter? Isn't this what you wanted?"

Kip gripped Cash by the back of the head, pulled his face toward the opening on Kip's arm. He pressed the bleeding wound to Cash's mouth, forced it past his lips and teeth until the boy had no choice but to open wide and let the black blood squirt and slide down his throat.

Once Kip finally released him, Cash scurried away on his back, his sneakers squeaking and splashing in the colorful mess of his former classmates. His skin changed from a fleshy pink color to maroon in seconds, then a dark purple, crisscrossed with black veins that pulsed and bulged. His cheeks expanded like he had a balloon in his mouth, and black liquid ran from his eyes, his nose and ears. Once his mouth opened, a waterfall of black blood exploded and sprayed all over his chest and stomach.

Then the front door flew open, and Kip locked eyes with Zak and Gwendolyn. His smile oozed into a scowl, and his hate went from hot to boiling.

Cash let out a tiny squeal just before his body erupted like a giant zit, splashing the inky blood all over the walls and floor and ceiling.

Zak screamed, fell onto his ass as he wiped at his eyes and spat. His face and torso were covered with Cash's blood, and he panicked and kicked his legs as he furiously wiped and clawed.

Gwendolyn did the same, and as Kip seized her, he slapped a fat hand to her mouth before she could scream, then began dragging her up the stairs toward his room.

It felt like someone had put out a cigar in each of his eyes, filled his mouth with boiling, rancid soup.

He couldn't help but scream as he used the heel of his palm to rub his eyes, pressing hard, kicking his legs as the pain refused to let up. Gwen had screamed too, and he knew she was right beside him, but he couldn't help her, couldn't reach out to make sure she was okay. His pain had his full attention, and he was sure that he was blind for life now, that whatever that liquid was that blew from Cash's expanded, inflated body had burned his eyes away, left him nothing but scorched sockets.

But even through his torture, Zak couldn't help but think about the nightmare he had walked into just before going blind.

Kip stood there, completely nude, his body wet and hairless and the color of a bruised corpse. Black blood ran down from his wounds, along with vivid purples and greens. His mouth pulled into a vast grin that had torn his upper and lower lips completely in half, revealing the black teeth and gums beneath.

Cash was on his back, his body bloated to the size of a small cow. It looked like he'd been pumped full of black juice until his skin was ready to rip from the pressure inside. His mouth was stretched wide, eyes rolling loosely in his sockets.

Just before he blew, Zak caught a quick glimpse of the others. Or what used to be them. They were little more than twitching limbs lying in a growing puddle of colorful liquid flesh. It looked like a mountain of melted ice cream, all flavors blended into a mess of color and cream. Bones clacked against the tile, a few screaming faces here and there emerging from the sloppy mound, though the only sound was sizzling and gurgling.

The pain began to subside slightly. Zak's panic subsided slightly, long enough to collect himself. He blinked, was able to see his hands, the doorstep.

I'm not blind. I still have my eyes.

Everything was still blurred around the edges, but he was thankful for any sight at all. They still burned, and his mouth still tasted like hot bile as if he'd just thrown up, but he was able to ignore it as he jumped to his feet, faced the house.

"Gwen? Are you all right?"

No answer.

Zak blinked some more, used the inside of his shirt to wipe at his eyes again. Things became a little more clear, but not by much. Clear enough for him to realize pretty quickly that Gwen was not there.

I heard her scream, but only for a moment before silence took over.

Zak already knew it was Kip. Kip had her, grabbed her while Zak was smothered in pain.

"Kip! You motherfucker!" Zak gripped the doorframe on both sides, poked his head in. *"Kip! What the fuck have you done!"*

The last time Zak had caught a glimpse of this classmates, there were still pieces of them whole. Now, he didn't even see bones. Just a huge puddle of color and blood, covering every inch of the floor, soaking into the living room carpet. The scent was like a honey-glazed ham baking in the oven, savory yet sweet, and Zak added to the growing puddle as a stream of vomit shot from his throat.

The only remaining corpse was Cash, who was still on his back, his body expanded to twice its girth, though blown wide open to reveal the tropical-colored viscera within. But even as Zak stared, it was melting like a glob of butter on a hot frying pan, slowly, foaming and sizzling.

The boy's face was frozen in a shriek of anguish, his face basted in Kip's black blood. The expression melted away into a featureless blob of liquid flesh and bone.

"Kip! Where are you, you fucking bastard!"

Right before Zak placed a foot into the thick muck on the floor, something hit him in the back of the head so hard, everything went black and his mouth tasted like metal. The side of his face hit the floor, splashed in the warm goop there. Zak only moaned and writhed for a second before flopping onto his back and facing the doorway.

Chuck smiled down at him.

Gwendolyn was heavier than she looked. And the way she flung her arms and kicked her legs, it was almost impossible getting her up the stairs, and even harder to get her up the attic steps and into his room.

But he got her there. She now sat on the floor, wiping the black from her eyes as she stared at the liquid puddle that used to be Jade Brewster.

Wow...I never thought in a million years I'd have Jade and Gwendolyn in my room. And at the same time!

Even though his body was numb, he could still feel the butterflies in his stomach as he stared down at Gwendolyn. The terror and revulsion knotting her face still didn't hide her beauty. She looked as gorgeous and perfect as ever, and Kip didn't know what else to do but sit beside her on the floor, rest his chin in his hands, and smile at her.

"Do you like my room? Do you know how many times I imagined you here with me?"

Gwendolyn crab-walked backwards away from him, her left hand plunging into the congealed puddle of Jade. She squealed and wiped the gooey substance off on her jeans, but kept crawling away until the back of her head hit the wall. Then she just sort of crumbled, hugged her knees and wept.

"I know," Kip said, remaining in his spot. "I know I'm disgusting. It's always been this way."

She didn't respond, didn't even look at him. Her whispery cries made Kip want to hold her, kiss her, tell her everything would be okay, that he would take care of her from now on. That she was his girl now.

But I can't make her love me. I'm all out of...

His eyes landed on the small plastic trash can sitting next to his standing mirror. Still overflowing with used tissue. Even from where Kip sat across the room, he could see the dried blood.

"Oh, Gwendolyn. We're going to be so happy together. Don't you see? It was always meant to be this way. We were supposed to be together." He crawled across the room, and when he shot a glance toward Gwendolyn, she was watching him now, her eyes covered in black, but red and puffy from crying. "You know? Maybe that's why all this happened. So we could be together. I mean…you're here now. In my room. Just like in my dreams. And that wouldn't be possible if none of this happened. It was worth it. Every one of those fucking assholes deserved it…don't you think?"

"Not like this, Kip," she said with a shaky voice, then sniffled and ran the back of her hand across her nose. "Nobody needed to die. All you had to do was ask. We could have hung out a long time ago. I've always liked you, Kip. I've always—"

"Hung out. We could have hung out. That's not what I wanted. You always liked me? Well…I always *loved* you. I don't want to hang out. *I want you to love me! I want you to love me the way I've always loved you. Not Zak!*"

Kip had his hands on the wastebasket now, pulled out a handful of tissues. He opened up the first one, and along with the blood, he found a few dried up globs of pus. Now petrified, but still powerful he hoped. Either way, Gwendolyn was going to eat it. She would eat it and then she would love him.

Her eyes fell on the ball of tissues squeezed in his fist.

"What are you doing?"

Kip walked toward her, his feet so full of fluid that they made a squishing sound with every step he took. As he grew nearer, his skin got to thrashing, inflating and deflating, spraying juice in all directions.

"I just want you to love me, Gwendolyn. That's all. Not anyone else. Just you."

She tried to jump to her feet and run away, but she slipped

in Jade, left her feet, landed hard on her side.

Kip didn't waste a second. He dove for her, crammed the tissue into her mouth. Then another. And another.

She fought, and though he couldn't feel a thing, it was nice to have her under him like that. His skin against her skin. Their flesh mending into one being.

"Kip?" she said, her voice high-pitched and dreamy.

"I'm here. I'll always be here."

"I…I need you."

Chuck's bullet wounds still leaked that black fluid in a steady drip as if there was no end to the stuff. His intestines looked ripped apart, almost as if some animal had gotten a hold of them. Chewed up and torn to ribbons.

"Toad is alive. Can you feel him?" When Chuck said this, his eyes circled in opposite directions. When they were done, one pointed at the ceiling, the other at the floor, yet he still seemed to be able to see Zak. "He's mine. Aaaaaall mine."

Zak stood, his back soaked in liquid flesh. The back of his head throbbed from the hit he took and his vision started to blur on him. But when Chuck stepped past the threshold and toward him, both hands outstretched, that fucking smile pulled as tight as it would go, Zak reached into his waistline and pulled out his pistol. Chuck stopped but only laughed, grabbed hold of a tube of intestine and began stroking it.

"What you gonna do with that?"

Zak let Chuck take a few more steps forward before he pulled the trigger. The bullet hit Chuck in the face, rocked his head back, splashed black over the wall behind him. He staggered but didn't fall, but Zak rushed forward, jabbed the barrel into Chuck's left eye, then pulled the trigger until it clicked empty.

Chuck fell this time, smacked the back of his ruined skull on the floor and splashed the multicolored liquid. The stuff soaked into Chuck's hair, matted it. His eye was a smoking mess of torn flesh and black.

But Chuck only giggled, waved his arms and legs and splashed. As he laughed, the black blood sprayed from his lips, rained back down onto his face and freckled it in ink.

"The Toad is miiiiiine!"

Zak grabbed hold of the rail by the stairs with one hand to steady himself, then lifted his foot as high as it would go before slamming it down into Chuck's face. He kept stomping, putting everything he had into each thrust. Blood and melted flesh splashed everywhere, slapped against Zak's face and torso, but he didn't let that slow him as he pummeled Chuck and roared as he did it.

Each stomp only made Chuck laugh harder, even when his skull caved in and crushed under the onslaught, his mouth still moved as if laughing, though the laughs themselves had become nothing more than gurgled choking sounds.

Zak stomped until Chuck's head was nothing more than a pile of meat, and still Chuck's arms and legs moved in lazy circular motions, a wet clicking sound rattling from his throat.

There was a commotion from upstairs. Coming from the attic. Loud bangs. As Zak stormed up the stairs, he tried to listen for Gwen's voice, maybe a scream, but only heard the occasional knock against the ceiling.

The attic steps were already down. Zak took them two at a time, fists as hard as marble, teeth clenched so his entire head hurt.

"Kip, don't you hurt her!" he screamed as he rushed into the room. But he stopped short. Stood there. His stomach dropped and his chest tightened. His knees went weak and he collapsed to the floor, shaking his head.

Kip and Gwen stood in the middle of the room. Holding each other. Gwen running her tongue across his chest and stomach and legs and groin, nibbling at his flesh and consuming the rainbow colors that flowed free. The stuff covered her face like yogurt, all flavors.

Her skin was already sizzling by the time she locked lips with Kip. Bubbles formed and popped, and the purple and green ooze burst out. Kip held her close, roamed her body with his chubby hands, their tongues swirling as they writhed against each other.

"Kip...Kip no..."

Kip pulled away from Gwendolyn, turned toward Zak. Black tears ran from his eyes, his skin in a frenzy as if thousands of birds were trapped within his body and trying to flap out.

Gwen's head rocked back, hung loose, dropped between her shoulder blades. Her face looked like purple custard, and as Zak stared at it, it slid off her skull and slapped the floor. Her hair burned away like dynamite fuses.

"We can't be together, Zak. Not here. There's only one way."

"K-Kip…wait…"

Kip dropped Gwen's molten body to the floor. He held her pistol, used the back his hand to wipe his tears as he watched Gwen continue to melt away. Her skull face rocked back and forth, as if she were still denying what was happening to her. What was left of her arms and legs knocked against the floor as she twitched, her body dissolving and spreading out. The iridescent puddle had just about reached Zak, and he stuck his hand out, ran his fingers through the hot liquid, his shoulders jumping as he wept.

Not just for Gwen, but for Kip. For himself.

"I loved her so much. You know that. I told you that." Kip had the gun pointed at Zak, gouts of slime falling from his hand. *"I fucking told you that, Zak!"*

Zak wanted to explain, let Kip know that nothing happened, that it was their concern for him that had brought them together in the first place. But he couldn't say that. Couldn't say anything. He just lowered his head and cried.

"How could you do this to me? You were the only friend I ever had…and you took her from me."

Zak shook his head, waited for the bullet to come.

"This is the only way. The only way we'll ever be together. She's worth it."

When the shot rang out, Zak thought he was dead. He didn't feel any pain, but he just knew it would show itself any second.

But it never did. Then there was a loud thump, and Zak uncovered his face.

Kip lay face-down on the floor, a black puddle spreading from his head. A ghost finger of smoke twirled from the gun's barrel.

"Kip...*Kip!*"

Zak crawled across Gwen's liquefied remains, the runny flesh soaking into his pants and searing his palms like hot grease. As he grew nearer, he saw the exit wound in the back of Kip's head. He hoped Kip would be like Chuck, hoped he would still be alive regardless of the mortal wound.

But when he reached Kip, lifted his head and laid it into his lap, he knew his cousin was dead.

He leaned over and touched his forehead to Kip's.

"I'm sorry, cousin. I'm so sorry."

EPILOGUE

Ernie snorted a line off the middle console, tilted his head back and enjoyed the drip. He checked the address one last time on Sarah's phone, then tossed it into the back. This was the place all right.

"Here I come, you little motherfucker."

He wouldn't kill Zak. Not yet. He wanted to drag him back home first, show him his mama. All the pieces of her. Piled up in the bathtub.

You wanted to leave me? Now look at you, you stupid bitch.

He was just going to shoot her, nice and clean. But her little fuck ass son took his pistol with him. So he had to use the ax he kept in the garage. Never knew why he bought an ax. Didn't have firewood to chop or anything. But the fucker sure came in handy last night.

He took one more line, then a long pull of his bottle of Jack before opening the driver's door and heading toward the house. The lights were on inside, and the front door was wide open. The only car in the driveway was Zak's POS, so he figured Sarah's sister wasn't home. Which was good. Not that he couldn't use a little pussy before his long drive back to California.

But he wanted this to be quick. In and out. Get that little fucker, knock his ass out, and get the fuck gone. If the little pipsqueak cousin was here, if he tried to interfere, it would be easy to get rid of him. He wouldn't kill him if he didn't have to, but it wouldn't make much of a difference either way.

Maybe I'll bring both the little fuckers with me.

He peered into the home, covered his nose and wrinkled his brow as he stared at the mess on the floor. Looked like a sea of melted candy or something, smelled like cooked meat. It turned his stomach, but he stepped into it anyway, cringing as the goo soaked into his tennis shoes.

It only took him a couple of minutes to check the first floor, but there was no sign of anyone. He almost called out, but bit his tongue, slowly and quietly made his way to the second floor. The first thing he saw was the attic, its foldout stairs lowered, a soft light glowing from inside.

And what is that noise? Crying?

He climbed the steps, peered into the small room. The floor was covered in the same liquid as downstairs, but something floated in it. He squinted, mouthed the words, "what the fuck?" without saying them.

A face floated by. It looked almost completely melted down, like it had been made of wax, but it still had eyeholes and a nose, though the nose was a messy stump of glistening flesh. The mouth was gone completely. Then he spotted a foot…and a hand, and as he stared at them, they dissolved, melted into the rest of the goop on the floor.

"Jesus."

When the word left his mouth, Zak turned and locked eyes with him. Ernie had been too caught up with the nasty shit on the floor to see the boy until they were already looking at each other.

Ernie climbed the last few steps, stood tall, pointed a hard finger at Zak. "You're dead, boy. Just like your mama."

And all Zak did was smile.

The smile shook Ernie, sent tremors through his bones. He even backed up a step, but the back of his shoe hit something.

"Hi, Chuck," Zak said.

"Wha—"

Strong hands seized Ernie's shoulders, spun him around. He stared into the face of what looked like roadkill. Black fluid spurted from the smashed face, and a tongue snaked out of the mess and spun in the air just before a stream of the black stuff rushed into Ernie's face and blinded him, sent hot lightning into sockets that scorched the optic nerves.

Ernie tried to shriek, but when his mouth opened, it was filled with more of the liquid. It rushed down his throat, set his belly on fire.

159

Then he was being dragged. He clawed at his eyes, hoping to god he wasn't truly blind.

He almost shouted with joy when a hint of light ignited in his vision, then the room started to come back into focus.

Zak stood over him. The boy's skin looked different, red, covered in pimples. Ernie didn't remember Zak ever having acne trouble before.

The living roadkill stood beside Zak, that tongue dancing like a cobra enticed by a snake charmer.

Zak held a bloated, purple corpse by its armpits, and once the boy lowered the corpse's head toward Ernie's face, he realized it was the pipsqueak. Zak's cousin. Recognized him from pictures that Sarah had hung in the living room back home.

What in the fuck is going on around here?

"Welcome to the party, Ernie," Zak said. "You're just in time."

Zak raked his nails across the pipsqueak's swollen face, rupturing the fat, greasy boils there. Purple and blue and green and pink poured from the opened flesh and coated Ernie's face, filled his mouth and nostrils and eyes.

And for the briefest of moments, just a flash, Ernie felt fantastic. Like he could fuck every woman in the world.

But that melted away into an inferno of pain and suffering as his flesh bubbled and started slipping off his body.

As Zak smiled down at him, the zits on the boy's face got to moving.

Pulsating.

Throbbing.

And then Ernie's eyes burst, and he let out a final scream before even that turned to liquid.

SHANE MCKENZIE is the author of *Infinity House, All You Can Eat, Bleed on Me, Jacked, Addicted to the Dead, Muerte Con Carne, Escape from Shit Town* (co-authored with Sam W. Anderson and Erik Williams), *Fairy, The Bingo Hall,* and many more to come. He is also the editor at Sinister Grin Press. He lives in Austin, TX with his wife and daughter. He's got plenty of pus for everyone, but it's first come first served. Don't be greedy.

BIZARRO BOOKS

CATALOG   SPRING 2013

ERASERHEAD PRESS

Your major resource for the bizarro fiction genre:

WWW.BIZARROCENTRAL.COM

Introduce yourselves to the bizarro fiction genre and all of its authors with the Bizarro Starter Kit series. Each volume features short novels and short stories by ten of the leading bizarro authors, designed to give you a perfect sampling of the genre for only $10.

BB-0X1
"The Bizarro Starter Kit"
(Orange)
Featuring D. Harlan Wilson, Carlton Mellick III, Jeremy Robert Johnson, Kevin L Donihe, Gina Ranalli, Andre Duza, Vincent W. Sakowski, Steve Beard, John Edward Lawson, and Bruce Taylor.
236 pages $10

BB-0X2
"The Bizarro Starter Kit"
(Blue)
Featuring Ray Fracalossy, Jeremy C. Shipp, Jordan Krall, Mykle Hansen, Andersen Prunty, Eckhard Gerdes, Bradley Sands, Steve Aylett, Christian TeBordo, and Tony Rauch. **244 pages $10**

BB-0X2
"The Bizarro Starter Kit"
(Purple)
Featuring Russell Edson, Athena Villaverde, David Agranoff, Matthew Revert, Andrew Goldfarb, Jeff Burk, Garrett Cook, Kris Saknussemm, Cody Goodfellow, and Cameron Pierce **264 pages $10**

BB-001 "The Kafka Effekt" D. Harlan Wilson — A collection of forty-four irreal short stories loosely written in the vein of Franz Kafka, with more than a pinch of William S. Burroughs sprinkled on top. **211 pages $14**

BB-002 "Satan Burger" Carlton Mellick III — The cult novel that put Carlton Mellick III on the map ... Six punks get jobs at a fast food restaurant owned by the devil in a city violently overpopulated by surreal alien cultures. **236 pages $14**

BB-003 "Some Things Are Better Left Unplugged" Vincent Sakwoski — Join The Man and his Nemesis, the obese tabby, for a nightmare roller coaster ride into this postmodern fantasy. **152 pages $10**

BB-005 "Razor Wire Pubic Hair" Carlton Mellick III — A genderless humandildo is purchased by a razor dominatrix and brought into her nightmarish world of bizarre sex and mutilation. **176 pages $11**

BB-007 "The Baby Jesus Butt Plug" Carlton Mellick III — Using clones of the Baby Jesus for anal sex will be the hip sex fetish of the future. **92 pages $10**

BB-010 "The Menstruating Mall" Carlton Mellick III — "The Breakfast Club meets Chopping Mall as directed by David Lynch." - Brian Keene **212 pages $12**

BB-011 "Angel Dust Apocalypse" Jeremy Robert Johnson — Meth-heads, man-made monsters, and murderous Neo-Nazis. "Seriously amazing short stories..." - Chuck Palahniuk, author of Fight Club **184 pages $11**

BB-015 "Foop!" Chris Genoa — Strange happenings are going on at Dactyl, Inc, the world's first and only time travel tourism company.
"A surreal pie in the face!" - Christopher Moore **300 pages $14**

BB-032 **"Extinction Journals" Jeremy Robert Johnson** — An uncanny voyage across a newly nuclear America where one man must confront the problems associated with loneliness, insane dieties, radiation, love, and an ever-evolving cockroach suit with a mind of its own. **104 pages $10**

BB-037 **"The Haunted Vagina" Carlton Mellick III** — It's difficult to love a woman whose vagina is a gateway to the world of the dead. **132 pages $10**

BB-043 **"War Slut" Carlton Mellick III** — Part "1984," part "Waiting for Godot," and part action horror video game adaptation of John Carpenter's "The Thing." **116 pages $10**

BB-047 **"Sausagey Santa" Carlton Mellick III** — A bizarro Christmas tale featuring Santa as a piratey mutant with a body made of sausages. 124 pages $10

BB-048 **"Misadventures in a Thumbnail Universe" Vincent Sakowski** — Dive deep into the surreal and satirical realms of neo-classical Blender Fiction, filled with television shoes and flesh-filled skies. **120 pages $10**

BB-053 **"Ballad of a Slow Poisoner" Andrew Goldfarb** — Millford Mutterwurst sat down on a Tuesday to take his afternoon tea, and made the unpleasant discovery that his elbows were becoming flatter. **128 pages $10**

BB-055 **"Help! A Bear is Eating Me" Mykle Hansen** — The bizarro, heartwarming, magical tale of poor planning, hubris and severe blood loss... **150 pages $11**

BB-056 **"Piecemeal June" Jordan Krall** — A man falls in love with a living sex doll, but with love comes danger when her creator comes after her with crab-squid assassins. **90 pages $9**

BB-058 **"The Overwhelming Urge" Andersen Prunty** — A collection of bizarro tales by Andersen Prunty. **150 pages $11**

BB-059 **"Adolf in Wonderland" Carlton Mellick III** — A dreamlike adventure that takes a young descendant of Adolf Hitler's design and sends him down the rabbit hole into a world of imperfection and disorder. **180 pages $11**

BB-061 **"Ultra Fuckers" Carlton Mellick III** — Absurdist suburban horror about a couple who enter an upper middle class gated community but can't find their way out. **108 pages $9**

BB-062 **"House of Houses" Kevin L. Donihe** — An odd man wants to marry his house. Unfortunately, all of the houses in the world collapse at the same time in the Great House Holocaust. Now he must travel to House Heaven to find his departed fiancee. **172 pages $11**

BB-064 **"Squid Pulp Blues" Jordan Krall** — In these three bizarro-noir novellas, the reader is thrown into a world of murderers, drugs made from squid parts, deformed gun-toting veterans, and a mischievous apocalyptic donkey. **204 pages $12**

BB-065 **"Jack and Mr. Grin" Andersen Prunty** — "When Mr. Grin calls you can hear a smile in his voice. Not a warm and friendly smile, but the kind that seizes your spine in fear. You don't need to pay your phone bill to hear it. That smile is in every line of Prunty's prose." - Tom Bradley. **208 pages $12**

BB-066 **"Cybernetrix" Carlton Mellick III** — What would you do if your normal everyday world was slowly mutating into the video game world from Tron? **212 pages $12**

BB-072 **"Zerostrata" Andersen Prunty** — Hansel Nothing lives in a tree house, suffers from memory loss, has a very eccentric family, and falls in love with a woman who runs naked through the woods every night. **144 pages $11**

BB-073 **"The Egg Man" Carlton Mellick III** — It is a world where humans reproduce like insects. Children are the property of corporations, and having an enormous ten-foot brain implanted into your skull is a grotesque sexual fetish. Mellick's industrial urban dystopia is one of his darkest and grittiest to date. **184 pages $11**

BB-074 **"Shark Hunting in Paradise Garden" Cameron Pierce** — A group of strange humanoid religious fanatics travel back in time to the Garden of Eden to discover it is invested with hundreds of giant flying maneating sharks. **150 pages $10**

BB-075 **"Apeshit" Carlton Mellick III -** Friday the 13th meets Visitor Q. Six hipster teens go to a cabin in the woods inhabited by a deformed killer. An incredibly fucked-up parody of B-horror movies with a bizarro slant. **192 pages $12**

BB-076 **"Fuckers of Everything on the Crazy Shitting Planet of the Vomit At smosphere" Mykle Hansen** - Three bizarro satires. Monster Cocks, Journey to the Center of Agnes Cuddlebottom, and Crazy Shitting Planet. **228 pages $12**

BB-077 **"The Kissing Bug" Daniel Scott Buck** — In the tradition of Roald Dahl, Tim Burton, and Edward Gorey, comes this bizarro anti-war children's story about a bohemian conenose kissing bug who falls in love with a human woman. **116 pages $10**

BB-078 **"MachoPoni" Lotus Rose** — It's My Little Pony... *Bizarro* style! A long time ago Poniworld was split in two. On one side of the Jagged Line is the Pastel Kingdom, a magical land of music, parties, and positivity. On the other side of the Jagged Line is Dark Kingdom inhabited by an army of undead ponies. **148 pages $11**

BB-079 **"The Faggiest Vampire" Carlton Mellick III** — A Roald Dahl-esque children's story about two faggy vampires who partake in a mustache competition to find out which one is truly the faggiest. **104 pages $10**

BB-080 **"Sky Tongues" Gina Ranalli** — The autobiography of Sky Tongues, the biracial hermaphrodite actress with tongues for fingers. Follow her strange life story as she rises from freak to fame. **204 pages $12**

BB-081 **"Washer Mouth" Kevin L. Donihe** - A washing machine becomes human and pursues his dream of meeting his favorite soap opera star. **244 pages $11**

BB-082 **"Shatnerquake" Jeff Burk** - All of the characters ever played by William Shatner are suddenly sucked into our world. Their mission: hunt down and destroy the real William Shatner. **100 pages $10**

BB-083 **"The Cannibals of Candyland" Carlton Mellick III** - There exists a race of cannibals that are made of candy. They live in an underground world made out of candy. One man has dedicated his life to killing them all. **170 pages $11**

BB-084 **"Slub Glub in the Weird World of the Weeping Willows"**
Andrew Goldfarb - The charming tale of a blue glob named Slub Glub who helps the weeping willows whose tears are flooding the earth. There are also hyenas, ghosts, and a voodoo priest **100 pages $10**

BB-085 **"Super Fetus" Adam Pepper** - Try to abort this fetus and he'll kick your ass! **104 pages $10**

BB-086 **"Fistful of Feet" Jordan Krall** - A bizarro tribute to spaghetti westerns, featuring Cthulhu-worshipping Indians, a woman with four feet, a crazed gunman who is obsessed with sucking on candy, Syphilis-ridden mutants, sexually transmitted tattoos, and a house devoted to the freakiest fetishes. **228 pages $12**

BB-087 **"Ass Goblins of Auschwitz" Cameron Pierce** - It's Monty Python meets Nazi exploitation in a surreal nightmare as can only be imagined by Bizarro author Cameron Pierce. **104 pages $10**

BB-088 **"Silent Weapons for Quiet Wars" Cody Goodfellow** - "This is high-end psychological surrealist horror meets bottom-feeding low-life crime in a techno-thrilling science fiction world full of Lovecraft and magic..." -John Skipp **212 pages $12**

BB-089 **"Warrior Wolf Women of the Wasteland" Carlton Mellick III** — Road Warrior Werewolves versus McDonaldland Mutants...post-apocalyptic fiction has never been quite like this. **316 pages $13**

BB-091 **"Super Giant Monster Time" Jeff Burk** — A tribute to choose your own adventures and Godzilla movies. Will you escape the giant monsters that are rampaging the fuck out of your city and shit? Or will you join the mob of alien-controlled punk rockers causing chaos in the streets? What happens next depends on you. **188 pages $12**

BB-092 **"Perfect Union" Cody Goodfellow** — "Cronenberg's THE FLY on a grand scale: human/insect gene-spliced body horror, where the human hive politics are as shocking as the gore." -John Skipp. **272 pages $13**

BB-093 **"Sunset with a Beard" Carlton Mellick III** — 14 stories of surreal science fiction. **200 pages $12**

BB-094 **"My Fake War" Andersen Prunty** — The absurd tale of an unlikely soldier forced to fight a war that, quite possibly, does not exist. It's Rambo meets Waiting for Godot in this subversive satire of American values and the scope of the human imagination. **128 pages $11**

BB-095 **"Lost in Cat Brain Land" Cameron Pierce** — Sad stories from a surreal world. A fascist mustache, the ghost of Franz Kafka, a desert inside a dead cat. Primordial entities mourn the death of their child. The desperate serve tea to mysterious creatures. A hopeless romantic falls in love with a pterodactyl. And much more. **152 pages $11**

BB-096 **"The Kobold Wizard's Dildo of Enlightenment +2" Carlton Mellick III** — A Dungeons and Dragons parody about a group of people who learn they are only made up characters in an AD&D campaign and must find a way to resist their nerdy teenaged players and retarded dungeon master in order to survive. **232 pages $12**

BB-098 **"A Hundred Horrible Sorrows of Ogner Stump" Andrew Goldfarb** — Goldfarb's acclaimed comic series. A magical and weird journey into the horrors of everyday life. **164 pages $11**

BB-099 "Pickled Apocalypse of Pancake Island" Cameron Pierce—A demented fairy tale about a pickle, a pancake, and the apocalypse. **102 pages $8**

BB-100 "Slag Attack" Andersen Prunty— Slag Attack features four visceral, noir stories about the living, crawling apocalypse.A slag is what survivors are calling the slug-like maggots raining from the sky, burrowing inside people, and hollowing out their flesh and their sanity. **148 pages $11**

BB-101 "Slaughterhouse High" Robert Devereaux—A place where schools are built with secret passageways, rebellious teens get zippers installed in their mouths and genitals, and once a year, on that special night, one couple is slaughtered and the bits of their bodies are kept as souvenirs. **304 pages $13**

BB-102 "The Emerald Burrito of Oz" John Skipp & Marc Levinthal —OZ IS REAL! Magic is real! The gate is really in Kansas! And America is finally allowing Earth tourists to visit this weird-ass, mysterious land. But when Gene of Los Angeles heads off for summer vacation in the Emerald City, little does he know that a war is brewing...a war that could destroy both worlds. **280 pages $13**

BB-103 "The Vegan Revolution... with Zombies" David Agranoff — When there's no more meat in hell, the vegans will walk the earth. **160 pages $11**

BB-104 "The Flappy Parts" Kevin L Donihe—Poems about bunnies, LSD, and police abuse. You know, things that matter. 132 **pages $11**

BB-105 "Sorry I Ruined Your Orgy" Bradley Sands—Bizarro humorist Bradley Sands returns with one of the strangest, most hilarious collections of the year. **130 pages $11**

BB-106 "Mr. Magic Realism" Bruce Taylor—Like Golden Age science fiction comics written by Freud, *Mr. Magic Realism* is a strange, insightful adventure that spans the furthest reaches of the galaxy, exploring the hidden caverns in the hearts and minds of men, women, aliens, and biomechanical cats. **152 pages $11**

BB-107 "Zombies and Shit" Carlton Mellick III—"Battle Royale" meets "Return of the Living Dead." Mellick's bizarro tribute to the zombie genre. **308 pages $13**

BB-108 "The Cannibal's Guide to Ethical Living" Mykle Hansen— Over a five star French meal of fine wine, organic vegetables and human flesh, a lunatic delivers a witty, chilling, disturbingly sane argument in favor of eating the rich.. **184 pages $11**

BB-109 "Starfish Girl" Athena Villaverde—In a post-apocalyptic underwater dome society, a girl with a starfish growing from her head and an assassin with sea anenome hair are on the run from a gang of mutant fish men. **160 pages $11**

BB-110 "Lick Your Neighbor" Chris Genoa—Mutant ninjas, a talking whale, kung fu masters, maniacal pilgrims, and an alcoholic clown populate Chris Genoa's surreal, darkly comical and unnerving reimagining of the first Thanksgiving. **303 pages $13**

BB-111 "Night of the Assholes" Kevin L. Donihe—A plague of assholes is infecting the countryside. Normal everyday people are transforming into jerks, snobs, dicks, and douchebags. And they all have only one purpose: to make your life a living hell.. **192 pages $11**

BB-112 "Jimmy Plush, Teddy Bear Detective" Garrett Cook—Hardboiled cases of a private detective trapped within a teddy bear body. **180 pages $11**

BB-113 "The Deadheart Shelters" Forrest Armstrong—The hip hop lovechild of William Burroughs and Dali... **144 pages $11**

BB-114 "Eyeballs Growing All Over Me... Again" Tony Raugh— Absurd, surreal, playful, dream-like, whimsical, and a lot of fun to read. **144 pages $11**

BB-115 **"Whargoul" Dave Brockie** — From the killing grounds of Stalingrad to the death camps of the holocaust. From torture chambers in Iraq to race riots in the United States, the Whargoul was there, killing and raping. **244 pages $12**

BB-116 **"By the Time We Leave Here, We'll Be Friends" J. David Osborne** — A David Lynchian nightmare set in a Russian gulag, where its prisoners, guards, traitors, soldiers, lovers, and demons fight for survival and their own rapidly deteriorating humanity. **168 pages $11**

BB-117 **"Christmas on Crack" edited by Carlton Mellick III** — Perverted Christmas Tales for the whole family! . . . as long as every member of your family is over the age of 18. **168 pages $11**

BB-118 **"Crab Town" Carlton Mellick III** — Radiation fetishists, balloon people, mutant crabs, sail-bike road warriors, and a love affair between a woman and an H-Bomb. This is one mean asshole of a city. Welcome to Crab Town. **100 pages $8**

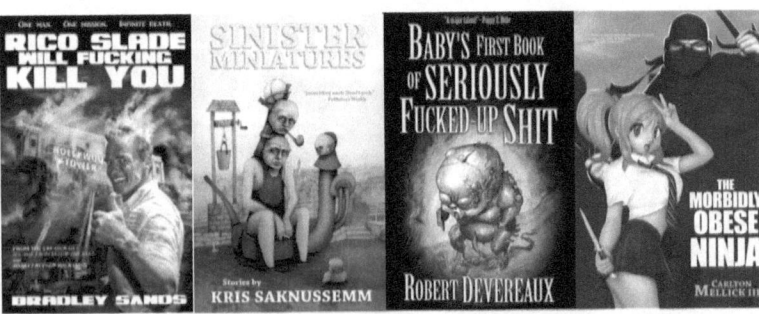

BB-119 **"Rico Slade Will Fucking Kill You" Bradley Sands** — Rico Slade is an action hero. Rico Slade can rip out a throat with his bare hands. Rico Slade's favorite food is the honey-roasted peanut. Rico Slade will fucking kill everyone. A novel. **122 pages $8**

BB-120 **"Sinister Miniatures" Kris Saknussemm** — The definitive collection of short fiction by Kris Saknussemm, confirming that he is one of the best, most daring writers of the weird to emerge in the twenty-first century. **180 pages $11**

BB-121 **"Baby's First Book of Seriously Fucked up Shit" Robert Devereaux** — Ten stories of the strange, the gross, and the just plain fucked up from one of the most original voices in horror. **176 pages $11**

BB-122 **"The Morbidly Obese Ninja" Carlton Mellick III** — These days, if you want to run a successful company . . . you're going to need a lot of ninjas. **92 pages $8**

BB-123 **"Abortion Arcade" Cameron Pierce** — An intoxicating blend of body horror and midnight movie madness, reminiscent of early David Lynch and the splatterpunks at their most sublime. **172 pages $11**

BB-124 **"Black Hole Blues" Patrick Wensink** — A hilarious double helix of country music and physics. **196 pages $11**

BB-125 **"Barbarian Beast Bitches of the Badlands" Carlton Mellick III** — Three prequels and sequels to *Warrior Wolf Women of the Wasteland.* **284 pages $13**

BB-126 **"The Traveling Dildo Salesman" Kevin L. Donihe** — A nightmare comedy about destiny, faith, and sex toys. Also featuring Donihe's most lurid and infamous short stories: *Milky Agitation, Two-Way Santa, The Helen Mower, Living Room Zombies,* and *Revenge of the Living Masturbation Rag.* **108 pages $8**

BB-127 **"Metamorphosis Blues" Bruce Taylor** — Enter a land of love beasts, intergalactic cowboys, and rock 'n roll. A land where Sears Catalogs are doorways to insanity and men keep mysterious black boxes. Welcome to the monstrous mind of Mr. Magic Realism. **136 pages $11**

BB-128 **"The Driver's Guide to Hitting Pedestrians" Andersen Prunty** — A pocket guide to the twenty-three most painful things in life, written by the most well-adjusted man in the universe. **108 pages $8**

BB-129 **"Island of the Super People" Kevin Shamel** — Four students and their anthropology professor journey to a remote island to study its indigenous population. But this is no ordinary native culture. They're super heroes and villains with flesh costumes and outlandish abilities like self-detonation, musical eyelashes, and microwave hands. **194 pages $11**

BB-130 **"Fantastic Orgy" Carlton Mellick III** — Shark Sex, mutant cats, and strange sexually transmitted diseases. Featuring the stories: *Candy-coated, Ear Cat, Fantastic Orgy, City Hobgoblins,* and *Porno in August.* **136 pages $9**

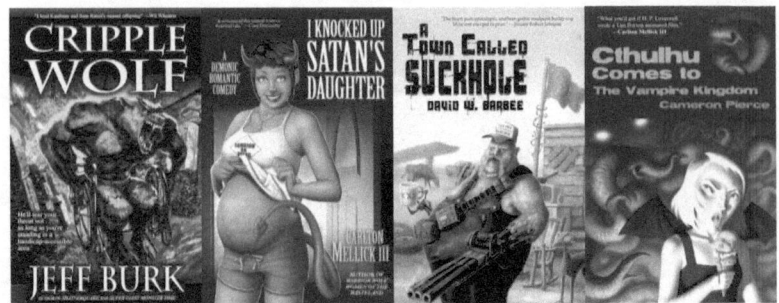

BB-131 **"Cripple Wolf" Jeff Burk** — Part man. Part wolf. 100% crippled. Also including *Punk Rock Nursing Home, Adrift with Space Badgers, Cook for Your Life, Just Another Day in the Park, Frosty and the Full Monty,* and *House of Cats.* **152 pages $10**

BB-132 **"I Knocked Up Satan's Daughter" Carlton Mellick III** — An adorable, violent, fantastical love story. A romantic comedy for the bizarro fiction reader. **152 pages $10**

BB-133 **"A Town Called Suckhole" David W. Barbee** — Far into the future, in the nuclear bowels of post-apocalyptic Dixie, there is a town. A town of derelict mobile homes, ancient junk, and mutant wildlife. A town of slack jawed rednecks who bask in the splendors of moonshine and mud boggin'. A town dedicated to the bloody and demented legacy of the Old South. A town called Suckhole. **144 pages $10**

BB-134 **"Cthulhu Comes to the Vampire Kingdom" Cameron Pierce** — What you'd get if H. P. Lovecraft wrote a Tim Burton animated film. **148 pages $11**

BB-135 **"I am Genghis Cum" Violet LeVoit** — From the savage Arctic tundra to post-partum mutations to your missing daughter's unmarked grave, join visionary madwoman Violet LeVoit in this non-stop eight-story onslaught of full-tilt Bizarro punk lit thrills. **124 pages $9**

BB-136 **"Haunt" Laura Lee Bahr** — A tripping-balls Los Angeles noir, where a mysterious dame drags you through a time-warping Bizarro hall of mirrors. **316 pages $13**

BB-137 **"Amazing Stories of the Flying Spaghetti Monster" edited by Cameron Pierce** — Like an all-spaghetti evening of Adult Swim, the Flying Spaghetti Monster will show you the many realms of His Noodly Appendage. Learn of those who worship him and the lives he touches in distant, mysterious ways. **228 pages $12**

BB-138 **"Wave of Mutilation" Douglas Lain** — A dream-pop exploration of modern architecture and the American identity, *Wave of Mutilation* is a Zen finger trap for the 21st century. **100 pages $8**

BB-139 **"Hooray for Death!" Mykle Hansen** — Famous Author Mykle Hansen draws unconventional humor from deaths tiny and large, and invites you to laugh while you can. **128 pages $10**

BB-140 **"Hypno-hog's Moonshine Monster Jamboree" Andrew Goldfarb** — Hicks, Hogs, Horror! Goldfarb is back with another strange illustrated tale of backwoods weirdness. **120 pages $9**

BB-141 **"Broken Piano For President" Patrick Wensink** — A comic masterpiece about the fast food industry, booze, and the necessity to choose happiness over work and security. **372 pages $15**

BB-142 **"Please Do Not Shoot Me in the Face" Bradley Sands** — A novel in three parts, *Please Do Not Shoot Me in the Face: A Novel*, is the story of one boy detective, the worst ninja in the world, and the great American fast food wars. It is a novel of loss, destruction, and--incredibly--genuine hope. **224 pages $12**

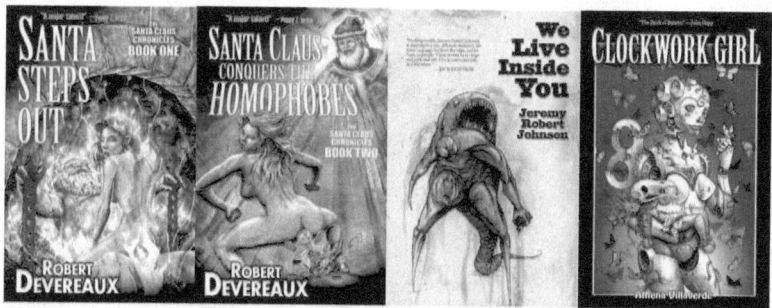

BB-143 **"Santa Steps Out" Robert Devereaux** — Sex, Death, and Santa Claus ... The ultimate erotic Christmas story is back. **294 pages $13**

BB-144 **"Santa Conquers the Homophobes" Robert Devereaux** — "I wish I could hope to ever attain one-thousandth the perversity of Robert Devereaux's toenail clippings." - Poppy Z. Brite **316 pages $13**

BB-145 **"We Live Inside You" Jeremy Robert Johnson** — "Jeremy Robert Johnson is dancing to a way different drummer. He loves language, he loves the edge, and he loves us people. These stories have range and style and wit. This is entertainment... and literature."- Jack Ketchum **188 pages $11**

BB-146 **"Clockwork Girl" Athena Villaverde** — Urban fairy tales for the weird girl in all of us. Like a combination of Francesca Lia Block, Charles de Lint, Kathe Koja, Tim Burton, and Hayao Miyazaki, her stories are cute, kinky, edgy, magical, provocative, and strange, full of poetic imagery and vicious sexuality. **160 pages $10**

BB-147 "Armadillo Fists" Carlton Mellick III — A weird-as-hell gangster story set in a world where people drive giant mechanical dinosaurs instead of cars. **168 pages $11**

BB-148 "Gargoyle Girls of Spider Island" Cameron Pierce — Four college seniors venture out into open waters for the tropical party weekend of a life-time. Instead of a teenage sex fantasy, they find themselves in a nightmare of pirates, sharks, and sex-crazed monsters. **100 pages $8**

BB-149 "The Handsome Squirm" by Carlton Mellick III — Like Franz Kafka's *The Trial* meets an erotic body horror version of *The Blob*. **158 pages $11**

BB-150 "Tentacle Death Trip" Jordan Krall — It's *Death Race 2000* meets H. P. Lovecraft in bizarro author Jordan Krall's best and most suspenseful work to date. **224 pages $12**

BB-151 "The Obese" Nick Antosca — Like Alfred Hitchcock's *The Birds*... but with obese people. **108 pages $10**

BB-152 "All-Monster Action!" Cody Goodfellow — The world gave him a blank check and a demand: Create giant monsters to fight our wars. But Dr. Otaku was not satisfied with mere chaos and mass destruction.... **216 pages $12**

BB-153 "Ugly Heaven" Carlton Mellick III — Heaven is no longer a para-dise. It was once a blissful utopia full of wonders far beyond human comprehension. But the afterlife is now in ruins. It has become an ugly, lonely wasteland populated by strange monstrous beasts, masturbating angels, and sad man-like beings wallowing in the remains of the once-great Kingdom of God. **106 pages $8**

BB-154 "Space Walrus" Kevin L. Donihe — Walter is supposed to go where no walrus has ever gone before, but all this astronaut walrus really wants is to take it easy on the intense training, escape the chimpanzee bullies, and win the love of his human trainer Dr. Stephanie. **160 pages $11**

BB-155 **"Unicorn Battle Squad" Kirsten Alene** — Mutant unicorns. A palace with a thousand human legs. The most powerful army on the planet. **192 pages $11**

BB-156 **"Kill Ball" Carlton Mellick III** — In a city where all humans live inside of plastic bubbles, exotic dancers are being murdered in the rubbery streets by a mysterious stalker known only as Kill Ball. **134 pages $10**

BB-157 **"Die You Doughnut Bastards" Cameron Pierce** — The bacon storm is rolling in. We hear the grease and sugar beat against the roof and windows. The doughnut people are attacking. We press close together, forgetting for a moment that we hate each other. **196 pages $11**

BB-158 **"Tumor Fruit" Carlton Mellick III** — Eight desperate castaways find themselves stranded on a mysterious deserted island. They are surrounded by poisonous blue plants and an ocean made of acid. Ravenous creatures lurk in the toxic jungle. The ghostly sound of crying babies can be heard on the wind. **310 pages $13**

BB-159 **"Thunderpussy" David W. Barbee** — When it comes to high-tech global espionage, only one man has the balls to save humanity from the world's most powerful bastards. He's Declan Magpie Bruce, Agent 00X. **136 pages $11**

BB-160 **"Papier Mâché Jesus" Kevin L. Donihe** — Donihe's surreal wit and beautiful mind-bending imagination is on full display with stories such as All Children Go to Hell, Happiness is a Warm Gun, and Swimming in Endless Night. **154 pages $11**

BB-161 **"Cuddly Holocaust" Carlton Mellick III** — The war between humans and toys has come to an end. The toys won. **172 pages $11**

BB-162 **"Hammer Wives" Carlton Mellick III** — Fish-eyed mutants, oceans of insects, and flesh-eating women with hammers for heads. Hammer Wives collects six of his most popular novelettes and short stories. **152 pages $10**